LULU PRESS

Not Another Christmas Carole

D.L. Meyer

Illustrations by
Valia Kapadai

October 25, 2010

Inspired by Charles Dickens' *A Christmas Carol.*

D.L. Meyer
PO Box 37
Luna Pier, MI 48157 – 0037
USA

Valia Kapadai
Ikoniou 11, Alsoupoli,
Nea Ionia - 14235
Athens, Greece

ISBN: 978-0-557-77322-0

Cover design: Valia Kapadai

To Bill Morris who said the holiday was just another day… until his "Carole" came along.

And to Leonard and Esther Tomanski who know how to keep Christmas well.

All my love.

Chapter 1

Foolish question, guys: 'What am I doing for the holidays?' The big, fat, pine-tree-in-the-window, sugar-on-the-cookie holidays?" Kat shook his head. "Lose the holly part. They're just *days* to me."

The question had come from two of Kat's closest friends but the answer was delivered into the depths of his beer.

Lolly and James Pelmutter exchanged looks over the bowl of bar nuts.

A string of electric chili peppers dangled over their booth; *Santa Baby* was playing on the jukebox; and Kat Thomas Petty was wallowing in woe-is-me's. Yep, it was beginning to look a lot like Christmas in Chug's Bar & Grill.

The woman pointed her chin at her husband, and then jerked her head at the man hunched to her right. It was couples' sign language and James knew it well. His eight months-pregnant wife was cuing him to speak their mind.

James slipped a finger into the neck of his shirt, pulling it away from his Adam's apple. "Aw, Jasper, don't say shit like that. Lolly here will think you're serious."

Kat glanced up and shuddered. James suspected he was reacting to the sound of his given name.

Kat had been Kat for as long as the trio could remember. But down at the public records office in Raintree and in the files at Saint Boniface parish, Kat was Jasper. No one, with the exception of Kat himself, remembered where the feline-sounding nickname had originated. It had been tripping off their tongues since their tag-playing days in Prospect Park.

Lately, however, Lolly had insisted that she and James jettison the friendly old moniker in favor of the more formal Jasper. As the due-date for their baby—Reginald Rudolph Pelmutter—drew near, she seemed determined to pay homage to the generations of parents before her who had chosen names for their offspring based on enthusiasm rather than sense.

"Really, Jasp," James tried again, "'tis the season, ya know? You're allergic, buddy. The tinsel, the mistletoe—it's all made in China. Lead content is probably too high in the paint. You always were the sensitive type."

Lolly sniffed. "Too sensitive."

Kat-Jasper tried to hide behind a deep swallow of brew. The name Carole hung unspoken in the air, midway between a burned out chili pepper and a tattered garland of foil letters spelling "Sea on G   tings". He faked a smile. "Sorry. It's not terminal. Really. A couple more weeks, I'll be over her. Promise." He twisted his torso to direct his next words to Lolly. "At present I've got a bit much of winter on my plate. The good news is you won't have to listen to my sad-sack ramblings much longer; I'm going to be heavily absent soon. There are only eight more shopping days until the big C. Considering all the not-so-merry shoppers I'll be dealing with next week, the only relaxation I'll want at the end of the day is to come home and kill things."

James laughed without thinking, earning him a second sniff from across the booth.

"About those not-so-jolly holidays…" he interjected.

Lolly rolled her eyes.

"Well, we *were* talking about that, weren't we?"

This time the wife smiled and patted her husband's hand. "What James is trying to say, Jasper, is we'd like you to join us for Christmas Eve dinner—and Christmas Day too, if you have room in your schedule."

It was Kat's turn to roll his eyes. "What a nice gesture, *Loleetah*. But I think not. You don't want a Grinch like me around to steal the happy out of your day."

The woman countered with a sugarplum lie. "Don't be silly. We want you with us. Besides, it's impossible to dampen our mood."

That's what Kat was afraid of. This year, he was determined to wallow in the debris of his latest shattered love affair: miserable, alone and unrepentant. No ho-ho-ho for him. He deserved to be bitter, damn it. *Why does it always happen in December? Always.*

"No thanks, Lolly."

"We're going to pretend we didn't hear that," the woman said, patting her swollen belly. "This is going to be a great Christmas. The best."

Kat gritted his teeth. "Lolly, no."

The woman opened her mouth again but James lifted one eyebrow. Sign language worked both ways. Lolly pressed her lips together and resigned herself to silence.

"If that's the way you want it, Kat," James said for her.

"Thanks, Jim. Yes. That's the way I want it."

Chapter 2

L olly was the designated driver for the evening. She had been the DD for the last eight months. James was the designated hoverer. Kat stood in the street near the front right bumper and watched as his burly friend adjusted the driver's seat as far back as it would go before tucking his wife behind the wheel. Then James smoothed down the "wings" of Lolly's jacket where the buttons no longer met across her belly. When he tickled her under the chin, she slapped playfully at his hand and beamed.

Make that double-chin now, Kat thought. He couldn't see Jim's face, but he was pretty sure the husband and wife were sharing a treacle-tart moment.

Ah, true love. Kat Petty tipped back his head to address a heaven he wasn't sure still existed. *I give it two more years. How 'bout you?*

"Give you a lift, Kat?"

His friend jogged between him and the front of the car, angling toward the passenger-side door. His hands were shoved deep inside his pockets, his feet pounding the pavement like pile drivers to ward off the cold already penetrating his work boots.

"No, thanks, buddy. I could use the air. One Blue Bull too many, I'm thinking."

Jim hesitated, his hand on the door latch. "You sure? It's

colder than a witch's tit out here."

With the car windows tightly closed, it was unlikely Lolly could hear him. She frowned just the same.

Kat grinned, and for the first time that night, it felt natural on his face. "That's what you'll be getting if you don't get in the car and tell her you invited me to Christmas dinner one last time."

Five years ago, James Pelmutter would have sneered at such a threat. Tonight, Kat's best friend since childhood only shrugged. "She means well, buddy. We both do. You shouldn't be alone all the time."

"I'm fine, Jim. Really. Just a touch of blues. I'm not alone *that* much. I do have friends besides you guys, you know."

"I'll be sure to tell her that." Jim yanked the door open and jumped inside as quickly as his large frame would allow. Still, the draft of air that slipped inside with him fogged the windows. Lolly raised a hand to wave good-bye. Jim lifted his hand too. But when Kat tossed back the salute, he realized his friend was only wiping away the condensation on his wife's window. He didn't even look Kat's way.

Nice of them to care about my being alone, seeing as how they're *the ones who left* me.

Turning up the collar on his ten-year-old Carhartt jacket, Jasper Petty moved off in the opposite direction from the vanishing car.

The two bars located at the end of Hide Street were closed. The three restaurants farther down had beaten them to it by hours. The pharmacy, the Albertsons, Franny's Fantabulous Flowers—all were dark. This was Chugwater, Wyoming, after all. "Open 24 Hours" was a myth here. Small town life, small town values: that was "real world" in Chug. Along with not-so-small-town hikes home in the dead of night. The city's taxi service called it a day when the sidewalks rolled up.

A snowflake drifted past Kat's face.

And then another.

Shit.

The plastic handle had snapped off his shovel during the closing storm of Winter 2010—and he'd neglected to buy a new one when Tractor, Farm & Fleet gave him the word to mark down his inventory. If these flakes piled up overnight, he'd be screwed getting his mother's aging pickup out of the garage and down the hill tomorrow.

His employees would laugh their asses off over that. Most of them were college kids from Cheyenne driving daddy-bought SUVs. For them, employment with TF&F was just "spending cash", so it didn't matter if they got there on time or not. For Mr. Petty, it meant a long walk through hip-high drifts to make sure the doors were unlocked and the lights were on precisely at eight.

Would it kill old-man Franklin to cruise in some snowy morning and help? Beamers have good traction, don't they? Wouldn't happen though. Franchise owners were invisible members of the staff. Collecting the profits, that's what they were good at. Sweat and worry were someone else's responsibility. Manager Petty's responsibility.

It wasn't supposed to be like this.

Kat had been the brightest of their triumvirate. James was fated to play football; then when he graduated—or not, as things turned out—he would join his father in his construction company. Lolly had set her heart on James and a pretty Cape Cod-style house in the Pelmutter subdivision out on Long Ranch Road, formerly Rural Route 8. She, too, had achieved her goals.

But Kat Thomas Petty had been smarter. Much smarter. Creative, said his composition teacher. Gifted, said the high school counselor. "College ma tear ee all," said his Da with pride. "The first in the Petty clan destined for State U." And the man had punctuated the prediction with tiny but regular deposits into a savings account he'd opened when Kat was still in grade school.

The flakes were falling harder now, piling up like the words in a Tolstoy novel.

This has freaking White Christmas written all over it.

Kat's steps slowed, but not from the weather. He glanced left, then right. The street was dark and empty. He cleared his throat.

"For most folks, snow was the tissue paper nature used to wrap up the holidays. For the thirty-four-year-old bachelor plodding along to nowhere, it was just one more freaking thing." His bare fingers began to tingle in his pockets. Was it from the cold, or the itch to be in front of his keyboard?

Sixteen years ago, Kat had dreamed of becoming a writer. Sixteen years ago, he'd entered—and won—a national short-story contest with a grand prize of ten-thousand smackers. It was much-needed cash, because it was also sixteen years ago that Kat learned his Da's meager earnings from the dairy co-op were still too high to qualify him for a college grant. His education nest-egg and prize winnings would cover his tuition but he'd have to work part-time for the room, board and books. That was fine with him. One day, he'd make his mark in the literary world. All authors had to pay their dues, Kat knew, and he was willing and able.

Then, the same sixteen years ago, his Da died.

Kat stopped walking and doubled over. The wound was as excruciating today as the moment he'd first heard the words "inoperable cancer." With the snow as a curtain, he sucked in three slow breaths, fought back the pain, straightened and moved forward again. The memory moved along with him. He picked at the scab as he walked.

"He had to know, Jasper," Doc Peterson had explained. "He just refused to admit it."

His mother had clung to Kat's arm a long time as the physician held up the x-rays and pointed out the areas of decay eating away at Lenny Petty's body. She'd clung to denial even longer, insisting that her man, her lover, her rock would show *them*. "Your Da will be home by Christmas," she had promised. And though he was eighteen and bright—the brightest of all his friends—Kat had dared to believe.

Leonard Lyle Petty died on December 22, 1992, his passing eased by drugs so strong he no longer knew the two people sitting vigil at his bedside: one begging, the other resigned.

There was no insurance. Lenny had chosen his son's education over possible disaster. And there were scant benefits from the co-op: a $9,000 payout from Wyoming Health & Life, courtesy of the statewide cattle workers association, followed by a guilt gift from the co-op's upper management equal to the amount of Lenny's last paycheck.

That, together with Kat's prize money and the salted-away college fund, brought his Da's estate to just over $28,000, barely enough to keep up the mortgage on the house for the next two years. Future house payments, utilities, food, car maintenance, gasoline, clothes: these things would have to be funded elsewhere.

Kat applied for the stock job at TF&F the Monday following the funeral, and was unloading trucks on Tuesday. His mom, to her credit, joined him in their struggle for survival. But having dropped out of school to marry Lenny when she was seventeen, she was ill-prepared for the workforce. Her minimum-wage job at the Suds & Duds Laundry/Dry Cleaners barely covered the fuel it took to get her there and back. To stretch their paychecks, Kat walked to work twice a week, weather permitting.

A gust of wind wrenched him back to the present. The snow had stopped being a Bing Crosby movie. It swirled along the street ahead of him like a dust devil, reminding him that sometimes he walked to work because weather and bald tires *insisted*.

Another half mile to go, all of it up hill. He could see the glow of the downstairs lights winking between blasts of snow. *At least she's home.* Maybe they could talk awhile before he retired to his pseudo apartment above the garage.

His mother had been spending a lot of time out lately. "Conversation and a little dinner," she had explained. "A chance to feel alive again."

Kat screwed up his face at her remembered words, and then spewed what he was thinking. "She's goddamn dating!"

The wind agreed and hissed its disapproval.

He would never say that out loud of course. He would never use that tone of voice with her either; she was his mother and he loved her. She knew what he was thinking though. Every firmly closed door and heavy footstep away from her must have seemed like a shout: "How can you, Mom? How can you?"

He was being unreasonable and he knew it. After all, she had mourned her lost husband for fifteen and a half years, and had visited his grave every Sunday for at least two of them. So what if the visits had trickled off to once a month? Then once a national holiday? And finally once a year? Kat had understood. She was healthy and, at 52, still young and attractive. She had many more years of life ahead of her. She couldn't and shouldn't spend them crying.

Still.

This year, just before Halloween, she had started flipping though magazines, asking Kat what he thought about hairstyles, dress styles, jewelry… "I mean, really, Kat. Could someone my age get away with *that?* I wouldn't look foolish, would I?"

Of course not, he had reassured her, not knowing what she was really asking.

Then she had begun to wear makeup again. To work.

Shortly after, the name Mark Hillard came up at dinner. Just a passing remark about a heavy package and the man's help getting it to the truck. The name surfaced again later that week while they watched a reality game show on TV. Mark, it seemed, would have known how to do such-and-so better than those silly dolts on the tube. When she spoke the name a third time, it was on their way to church that weekend and it was directed at a chubby balding man striding along the sidewalk.

"Look. There's Mark!"

The excitement in her voice had been unmistakable and she must have known it. Her next statement was quieter, more controlled. "*You* know, dear. That's the gentleman I mentioned: the technician who's been supervising the new equipment installation at work."

"A repairman," Kat jeered now.

The wind sneered with him. The branches above him tsked.

Oh come on, Kat. Be fair. His Da hadn't been much more than a hired-hand himself. And Lenny would have wanted his cherished "Evie" to be happy. Mark Hillard's attentions were a good thing. A little conversation and dinner now and then? What did it hurt if it made his mother smile?

But it did hurt. A lot.

At least she's home tonight.

Kat needed someone to talk to, and while his mother wasn't always the most sympathetic of souls when it came to his love life, she would be willing to listen before launching into a lecture about his bad choices... before she called Carole a woman of questionable morals… before she labeled him naïve for believing "a girl like that" was worth the time he'd lavished on her.

"Jasper, dear, you really should be more discriminating. Surely there are a few nice girls left in Chugwater? A lady or two who will appreciate what you have to offer?"

Nice girls? Ladies? Under the age of fifty? In Chugwater? Okay, there *had* been a few, back when he was in high school. But the better ones got married not long after turning in their caps and gowns. The best ones went away to college and never came back. Each year since, the herd had thinned. Then at the stroke of midnight on January 1, 2004, Kat had looked around and noticed something disquieting. Everyone at the New Year's Eve party was a couple.

Except him.

All the finest fillies had been systematically winnowed out by men with more time, more money and more game— leaving Kat the slim pickins: a love life that had degenerated into a steady stream of Caroles.

Okay, okay, don't exaggerate.

To be honest, only three of his old girlfriends had actually been named Carole. The first—Caroline, with a tiny circle over the i—had been self-centered. The second—Carol pronounced with a *Cahr* instead of a *Cair*—had been self-absorbed. By fate or Kat's bad judgment, both women had been schemers. He had counted his losses and moved on, making plans for dinner, a movie or whatever with other ladies from work, church or the extended families of well-meaning friends.

But from first to last, they had all turned out to be Caroles.

Pretty Caroles; plain Caroles; skinny Caroles; stubby, loud, shy Caroles; redheaded, blonde and brunette Caroles; long, short, smart and dumb Caroles. Yes, they looked different.

They even claimed to have different names. But they were all the same woman, over and over again: a self-serving predator that could identify a patsy at twenty paces. Kat seemed incapable of avoiding her, or of seeing behind her many masks.

"Is it me, Mom," he asked the growing storm. "What exactly *do* I have to offer?"

So, okay, he wasn't all that old yet and he still had his looks. Every one of his quick-burning flames had told him so; had commented on his turquoise eyes and boyish smile. He was well-read too, though they didn't seem to care. Once, he had mentioned Jean Auel to a date and she had asked, "Who's he?" Another time, he'd brought up *Simulacra and Simulation* hoping to discuss the book's impact on the movie *The Matrix*. (What had he been smoking, for heaven's sake!) The woman's eyes had glazed over.

The following weekend when he'd called that particular Carole for a date, she had changed her voice and pretended to be her roommate. "Carole... *(or Lisa or Cybil or whatever the hell her name had been)* ...is out for the evening. Would you like to leave a message?"

Why bother? He'd gotten *her* message loud and clear, if a bit nasal and high-pitched.

Apparently, Kat was good in bed too. All of his Caroles had slept with him the first night, and had continued to do the deed with him, moaning and writhing with enthusiasm, right up until the moment they altered the pitch of their voices and pretended to be someone else.

His mother would say they'd been someone else all along. Kat just hadn't been sharp enough to notice.

Carole Anne Wylie had been the most devious. On their first date three months ago, she had actually told him she would leave him one day. "I don't know what I want yet," she had warned him with disarming honesty. Her old BF had been a monster and Kat was a welcome relief. But he was just a respite; he should not think for one second that they were a permanent thing. Hell, she hadn't even tried to pretend she was interested in his writing or in the over one hundred novels that lined the walls of his studio apartment. She was "in transition" and if Kat could accept that, she would enjoy his company. And his bed, of course.

When she started making plans to go away for the holidays—and made no mention of inviting him along—he realized he was yesterday's news.

"Took you that long, eh?"

Kat mounted the steps to his mother's porch and pulled out his key ring.

"Real smart, kid. Smart as a blow to the head with a crowbar."

And in December. Again.

Well good riddance to her. At least he didn't have to buy the wench a gift.

His key stuck in the lock. "Damn." It was frickin' cold outside and his fingers were numb. He pulled the key out to insert it a second time but the ring slipped from his hand, landing with a jingle on his mother's Merry Christmas welcome mat.

Sure. Rub it in why don't you?

Bending over, he snatched up the circlet, and then straightened.

A man with silver flowing locks peered at him from the door window.

Chapter 3

C ome in, come in," the man urged, throwing the door open so hard it rattled the family photos peering down from the foyer wall. "Kat, right? Must be colder than a witch's tit out there. Get the hell inside, boy, before she frosts your balls."

Kat wasn't sure what to react to first: a stranger's presence in his mother's home, or the sound of Jim's words echoing back at him.

He opted for the former. "Who. Are. *You?*"

The man smiled, stretching a web of wrinkles upward to the corners of his eyes. In truth, his entire figure seemed wrinkled, from his badly knotted red tie to the rumpled black suit that hung on his skinny frame. Even the red socks that sagged beneath the cuffs of his pants looked wrinkled, as though his ankles were too thin to hold them up.

"We'll get to who I am in a minute," he assured Kat. "Just get your butt in here before it cracks from the cold." A pair of bony hands batted at Kat's hair and shoulders before spinning him around. Drifts of snow fell to the floor in slushy piles. Then the man slapped him on the ass.

"Too late. Looks like it's cracked already!"

"Hey! What the hell do you think you're doing?"

The bony hands spun him about again. This time, the eyes that stared into his were solemn. "Almost right, Kat. The question really is: 'What the hell is *Jasper Thomas Petty* doing?'"

Kat felt the door swing closed behind him. He heard the lock click softly. He saw the ruby-glass lamp inherited from Great Grandma Petty flicker to life in the parlor to his right. All the while, the man's hands remained curled around Kat's biceps.

"Holy shit," Kat said softly.

"That it is, my boy. That it is. Holier than thou. And it don't stink none either."

Blood rushed from Kat's head, searching for the shortest route to his toes. It was cut off from its goal when his knees collapsed. He would have folded like an accordion to the floor if the man hadn't tightened his hold on his arms. "Whoa, little buddy. Breathe, breathe."

Kat's boots thudded against the linoleum as he struggled to regain his footing. "Mom!" he hollered. "Mom, are you okay?!"

The man before him pursed his lips and tilted his head to the side. "Now why would I want to hurt a lovely old broad like your mum, hmm? I'm disappointed in you, boy. Sorely disappointed."

Kat dug in his heels and stiffened his spine. His balance returned and he thrust his hands forward to shove the intruder away.

It was like slamming his palms against concrete. The man stood firm. The only thing that moved was the guy's head as it returned to its full and upright position. "Not particularly friendly, are you?" he noted with a sniff.

For a moment, Kat swore he saw Lolly's plump face and turned-up nose.

"You did."

"I did what?" Kat whispered.

"See Lolly."

"Uh?"

"You'll see a lot more folks before I'm done with you."

The man released his grip on Kat's arms. "All better now? Good. Now let's get those wet clothes off before you catch your death." He reached for the zipper on the Carhartt jacket but Kat lurched away. "Independent squirt, ain't ya? Always gotta do things the hard way. Okay, suit yourself." A rumble of laughter erupted from his mouth. "Or *un*suit yourself, as the case may be." Bending over, the man slapped his knee. "Oh baby, I slay myself. I surely do."

Then the man straightened and stepped back out of the tiny foyer and into the center hall that split the Petty homestead in two. Crossing his arms, he shifted his weight to one hip, crossed his ankles and leaned to the side. It was the pose of a man completely at ease, resting against a wall, waiting for the next thing to take his fancy.

Only there wasn't any wall.

The skinny stranger stood before Kat, canted to one side, with no visible means of support to hold him up. Just air. And a cocky wag of his eyebrows that said, *Yes, my boy, I can.*

"I got a million of 'em, kid. The show's just starting."

Kat thought of his mother again and a knot of fear twisted in his throat. He struggled to call past it. "Mom?"

"She's fine, Jasper. She's not even here."

"What have you done with her?" *If he's hurt her…*

"I said she's fine," the man soothed. "I'd never hurt her, so hyper down. I like Evelyn. Everybody likes Evelyn. Too bad you don't take after her more."

Kat stretched his neck to glance through the archway to the parlor. The part of the room that he could see was empty and there were no moving shadows on the wall to indicate a presence.

"She's not here, Jasper."

Kat stepped to the right and placed his palm on the woodwork framing the parlor entry. A shift of his shoulders allowed him to lean out around the stranger and peer into the hall beyond. The kitchen at the far end was dark. The dining room door to the left was closed.

"Mom!"

"Want to use the phone? It's still working. For now, anyhow. Storm's going to take it out in an hour and twelve minutes. Should be fine for the moment. Just a little static. Your mom is at Mark's place. I put a bug in his ear a couple of hours ago to invite her over. He picked her up about the same time you were ordering your third beer at Chug's do-drop-inn."

Kat stiffened. "You're a friend of Mark's?"

The man stiffened too, in perfect imitation. "Am I a friend of Mark's?" he replied through tight lips, mimicking Kat's disdain. "You betcha. And Evelyn's friend. And James's friend. And Lolly's. And old man Franklin's." Stepping forward, he laid a hand on Kat's shoulder. A ripple of warmth flowed from his fingers through the double layer of tufted nylon, through the spun batting and quilted cotton lining, through Kat's flannel shirt, through his shivering skin and to the prickly soul beneath. "I was your Da's friend too when he was alive. And I would be your friend as well, if you'd stop putting up so many freakin' barriers."

Kat staggered away a second time, this time lurching sideways into the red glow of the parlor. "Stop that. Stop all of this. Who *are* you?!"

The man followed him into the room, smoothing his tie and adjusting his lapels. "Well, now. That's sort of hard to say. Pagan cultures claimed I was the sun god, Sol Invictus or—as Anglo Saxon warriors called me—Mithras. The Greeks referred to me as Christos, which if you have to be literal about it, means 'the anointed one'. Awfully stuffy for my tastes, though, so I seldom bring it up. This time of year, Christians think of me as the infant form of Yeshua. Hindus might argue I am much more like Lakshmi, the Goddess of Wealth."

The man halted, pointing to a newspaper on the hall table, its pages bulging with shopping circulars. "One look at that, and it would be hard to argue with them." Shaking his head, he tossed his arm across Kat's shoulders, and turned him toward the center of the room. "Now, in Germany, I was called Saint Nicholas," he continued with enthusiasm. "And in Great Britain folks might say I am the embodiment of St. Stephen, the patron saint of Boxing Day, but then we'd have to get into that whole meshuggahna thing about how Boxing Day really started, like was it a day for distributing boxes of fruit to trades people, a chance for the lord of the manor to distribute an annual allotment of durable goods to his serfs, the collection of alms in boxes by the clergy to help the needy…? I could go on and on, but I gotta tell ya, Kat, it hurts my head."

Without quite knowing how he got there, Kat floundered backwards into the red velvet settee left over from his Aunt Sophie's estate sale. The man did not join him. Instead he paced back and forth like a doddering old professor lost in a favorite lecture. "To the Buddhists, I'm Buddha; to the Sikhs, I'm Guru Nanak; and to the Jews I am the Messiah—but I haven't arrived yet." Pivoting suddenly, he threw his arms wide and waggled his fingers like a sideshow magician. A fire snapped to attention in the fireplace. The sconces flanking the archway flickered to life. "And thanks to Charles God-Bless-Us-Every-One Dickens, I have to do that whole Ghost of Christmas Past, Present and Yet-to-Come shtick." He dropped his arms. A choir of children's voices filled the air.

"Parlor tricks," he complained. "Nothing but parlor tricks." Glancing around, he bent low, snorted loudly, and slapped his knee as he had in the foyer. "Parlor tricks in the parlor. Am I good, or what?"

When he straightened, the singing faded away, along with his goofy grin. "Who do *you* think I am, Kat?"

I think you're not really here, was Kat's first thought.

Buddha/Guru Nanak/Messiah pinched Kat's cheek.

"Ow!"

"Want to rethink that, kid?"

"You're *not* here. You can't be. If I had to give you a name at all, I'd say you're Blue Bull Number Six."

Mithras spun around on the heel of one foot, giggling like a child. The bull horns on his headdress carved circles in the air. "Good one! Wish I'd thought of it."

"Or maybe that greasy hamburger," Kat muttered under his breath.

"Ah," St. Stephen mused, the ends of the horns coming together to form a halo. "A 'bit of undigested beef', hm? By the way, who did you like in that role: Alistair Sim or George C. Scott? Personally, I pick Henry Winkler for the win. I mean, the Fonz as Scrooge? How can you beat that?"

Kat's head was beginning to spin and the fire in the fireplace was heating the room past his comfort point. Fumbling with the zipper of his jacket, he plucked at the garment in a losing battle to take it off. With no further effort, it disappeared.

"Guest closet or upstairs bedroom?" Lakshmi asked, her voice soft and lilting. One of her eight arms held the jacket on an outstretched finger. A second arm snaked toward the hallway while another pirouetted upward. "I'd hang it in that old armoire in your apartment over the garage," she added, a fourth arm weaving to the left. "But when the heat goes out later tonight, you'd have to hike over there to get it. Bad planning."

"Stop! I mean it. Stop!" Squeezing his eyes shut, Kat covered his ears with his hands. For a second, he almost chanted, "Nana nana naaa naaa...I can't hear you."

Silence followed. Kat counted to twenty and opened one eye.

The man in the rumpled black suit stood quietly in the center of the room. "All done now?"

Kat lowered his hands and opened his other eye. Lifting his chin, he took a deep breath and said the obvious. "I think you're me."

The man smiled and nodded. "Pretty much. But you can call me Chi."

Chapter 4

C hi? Chi?" Kat murmured, his forehead creased. "I've heard that somewhere before."

"I should hope so," the man admonished. "Old lady Bandwell will be crushed if I have to tell her you forgot."

Clara Bandwell? His Sunday school teacher? The skinny tree-tall woman who told such wonderful stories? The old woman who died at least a dozen years ago? Kat's brows dipped together but he soon shook off the memory. "Wait, you're trying to distract me."

"That so?"

"Yeah," he insisted, leaping to his feet. "Where is my mother? How are you doing these... these... things? How do you know Clara Bandwell? How did you know what Jim said when we left Chug's?" He stalked forward, hands clench at his sides. "Tell me now or I swear, I'll pound you until you're nothing but a stain on the carpet."

Chi shook his long silver hair and raised his hands palms out to ward off Kat's anger. "Whoa, boy, whoa."

Kat spun away. "Mom!" he bellowed to the room, to the house, to his suddenly shaky world.

The aging wall phone in the kitchen rang in answer.

Chi laid a gentle hand on the young man's shoulder. "She's fine, Jasper. Talk to her. You'll see."

Kat shook off the hated sympathy and raced into the hall

toward the dark kitchen. The phone repeated its summons. "Mom," he cried, even before he could fumble the receiver to his ear. "Mom?"

"Hello, dear." Her voice crackled through a whisper of static. "You got home okay I see. Did Lolly and James bring you? The weather is turning nasty. I began to worry."

"Mom!" he interrupted. "Where *are* you?"

He could almost hear her blush. "Well, now, I'm at Mark's, dear. Nothing to worry about on my account." She cleared her throat. "He made too much dinner and didn't want to eat it all alone. See? No reason to fret."

Kat gripped the handle of the receiver with so much force the plastic seams creaked beneath his fingers. "Mom?"

Several seconds passed in silence, neither of them knowing what to say.

"Sweetheart," she finally sighed. "Sweetheart, dearest. You're still my best friend." Silence fell again, tainted by the hiss of snow on the line. "You always will be."

Kat pressed his head against the wall, cradled the phone to his face, and fought back tears. "Well, sure, Mom. I know that. It's just…"

Words failed him. *And me an author wannabe.* "I came home. You weren't here. No note…"

"You didn't see it?" she interjected, panic in her tone. "I put it on the dining room table… with a sandwich… you always come home hungry. I thought, 'He won't miss it there…' Oh, Kat…" Her own tears rose in her voice. "I'm so sorry. You must have been frantic. I didn't think…"

"It's okay, Mom," he soothed, feeling better than he had for many minutes. "Just so I know you're all right. Chi told me that's where you were but I wasn't sure I could trust him… Who is he, anyway? A friend of Mark's?"

The second silence was longer and deeper.

"Who, dear?"

The static rose to a roar.

"Chi, Mom… Mark's friend." He had to shout to hear himself over the sound barrier. "The guy who was here when I got home. Scrawny. Sixtysomething. A bit daft," he added, trying to laugh.

"Kat?" she answered, though it was obvious she wasn't answering him at all. "I think the storm is doing a number on Ma Bell. I can barely hear you."

"Mom! Who is this man? When will you be home? When is Mark bringing you? I'll wait up."

"Oh dear," she mumbled. "He didn't know I was here. And now the connection is going bad…"

A deeper voice rumbled something in return and the line thudded twice as the receiver changed hands.

"Jasper?" called Mark Hillard. "I hope you can hear me, guy. Your mom is safe and sound. I've fed her, though not as good as she deserves." He chuckled, but not to Kat. "The storm is cranking up so I'm going to put her in my guest room. Safe and sound, Jasper. Okay, buddy? Kat?"

Evie's son said nothing. Really, what could he say? She was an adult. The weather was bad. Mark was a church-going man and Evelyn Petty had a history of choosing a good man as her companion. She was moving on and Kat was being left behind. Again.

"Jasper?!" The line thudded once more. "I think I lost him, Evie. Hope he heard me…" The static cut out. The receiver grew heavy. Mark had rung off.

A bony hand took the phone from his fingers and placed it back in its base on the wall. "He *is* a good man, Kat. One of the best. A gentleman. He won't lay a finger on her that she doesn't want." For a moment, Kat thought he was hearing his Da's voice, but of course that couldn't be. "She couldn't have picked a better second husband if I'd done it myself."

An arm circled his shoulder, and that warmth he'd felt flowing from Chi's fingers earlier filled Kat's chest, almost melting the cold in his heart.

"Mark Hillard loves Evelyn Petty," the voice continued softly. "But he won't sleep with her. Not tonight. And not tomorrow night. Or any night until they marry. Old-fashioned. Both of them. A wonderful match. Wonderful."

The arm turned Kat away from the darkened kitchen and back toward the hall.

"He'll propose on Valentine's Day. 'I bit hasty,' he'll tell her—down on one knee—'but we aren't getting any younger, love.'"

Kat exhaled noisily, his footsteps stuttering to a stop just outside the dining room door.

"She'll cry," Chi soothed. "The happy ones always do. They'll have more than twenty-nine blissful years together before a heart attack takes Mark in his sleep on August 12, 2047."

The arm around Kat's shoulder tightened. "She'll lean on you a lot then, Kat. Like she did before. The only thing I don't know is will you be there for her the way she needs? Or will you just prop her up again?"

The door to their right opened slowly, the room beyond it lit with a soft glow that didn't come from any lamp that Kat could see. The sandwich his mother had made sat at the end of their dining table on a china plate with a silver-gilt edge, a plate Kat had never seen before. It rested on a damask tablecloth edged in lace—a cloth he'd never laid eyes on in his life. Heavy platinum silverware flanked it. A crystal goblet filled with milk stood beside it. Candles flickered in an elaborate candelabrum. The children's choir was singing softly in the walls.

"By night's end, though," Chi concluded with a quick squeeze and release of Kat's shoulders, "I will know the answer to those questions. We'll both know."

A light shove in Kat's back sent him stumbling toward the late-night supper. "So eat up, kid. You're going to need it."

Chapter 5

W hat is all this? These aren't my mother's things."

Chi did a jaunty quick step to an armchair on the table's far side. "Actually, they are. Or they would have been, had Evelyn's Grandmother Iris passed them down." The chair slid away from the table under its own power. The man settled into it, his long legs stretched before him, ankles crossed. Scratching at his chin, he pursed his lips in distaste. "Never liked that woman. Thought if she couldn't take it with her, no one else should have it either. Sold everything of value before she died. Sad. Very sad."

Kat approached the place-setting cautiously.

"It won't bite ya," Chi teased.

Kat eyed him with suspicion, the shadow of a thought darkening his face. "The Ghost of Christmas Past, you said. That's what this is, isn't it. You're trying to teach me a lesson. Your name: Chi. It's short for Christmas, right?"

The man's facial features scrunched together as though he'd swallowed a bug. "God forbid. And you're missing a letter. No 'r' in Chi."

Kat nodded. Finally, he had this pegged. Gesturing to his own chair, he waited for the man to pull another magic trick out of his ass.

Chi wrinkled his nose and lisped a response. "You're on your own, you thilly thavage."

"Not particularly friendly, are you?"

"Like you said, I'm you."

"But only sort of."

"Now you're catching on." Chi reached across the table and picked up a wedge of Kat's mother's sandwich. She had cut it into quarters, something she hadn't done since he was a toddler. "You gonna eat this?"

"Make yourself to home." Kat yanked his chair out and spun it around so he could straddle it backwards. "You've done a pretty good job of that so far."

With his pinky finger extended, Chi bit daintily into the bit of white bread, bologna, mayo and tomato. "Mmm. Delicious." Then he waved at Kat's position on the seat. "More barriers, Kat? Not gonna make this easy are you?"

Kat wrapped his arms around the chair back and leaned in for battle. "Come on, give. Either you are a dream or you're an alcohol-induced hallucination. Doesn't matter which. I'm experiencing it and only I can end it."

Popping the remnant of sandwich into his mouth, Chi dusted his hands together and nodded as he chewed. "Now you're getting it," he mumbled, spraying crumbs onto the table. "Only you can end it. Remember that. It could speed things up here."

Kat nodded in return. "Okay. Let's start with your name. Why does it sound familiar to me?"

"You'll have to field that one, kid. Why *does* it sound familiar to you?"

"Mrs. Bandwell."

Chi lifted a finger. "Actually, *Miss* Bandwell. She lied about being a widow for years. There was no Mr. Bandwell. Old biddy was a spinster from Omaha."

Kat shook his head and made a fist. "Why do you keep doing that?" he growled, pounding the chair back. "If you are some kind of deity, shouldn't you be more respectful of people? Shouldn't you be watching your language and… and… acting more… I don't know. Like—well—like a *god*, damn it!"

The man in the black suit rose to his feet, placed his palms on the table and leaned forward. Way forward. His face came perilously close to Kat's. "I've been doing that for your entire thirty-four years, Jasper Thomas Petty." His silver hair rose in a cloud of static and the children in the walls stopped singing. "It didn't make an impression."

Kat shivered as a cold draft crawled up his spine. It did nothing to dampen his fighting mood. "But if you are all powerful, you should be able to do anything—even reform a recalcitrant jackass like me."

Chi tipped his head to the side and lifted his eyes to the ceiling. "Now ain't he a peach? Doesn't leave a god much of a choice, does he?" Straightening again to his full height, the man scrunched up his nose, twisted his mouth to the right, and then to the left. "How the hell did Elizabeth Montgomery do this?" Squeezing his eyes shut, and crossing his arms over the top of his head, he bent slightly from the waist and grunted.

Five quick notes twinkled in the air—B flat, G, B flat, G, B flat—highlighted by a touch of piano vibrato. Chi twitched his nose like he was Samantha Stevens.

After that, all hell broke loose.

Two streaks of lightening turned the glass in the dining room windows blue and then white. A double explosion of thunder followed. Kat leaped to his feet a millisecond before the items on the table rose in a whirlwind. The chair he'd been sitting on crashed into the wall. The flames on the candles roared toward the ceiling, licking at the chandelier until its brass arms drooped. Bits of molten metal dripped down, splashing off the flying silverware, the plate, the goblet. The milk that had been contained in the glass now squirmed like an amoeba in the wind. The sandwich fell apart, restacked itself, then fell apart again, over and over as it ran a race around Kat's head. The voices in the wall wailed a sinister "Alleluia".

Chi's clothing began to glow, the black suit dissolving to nothing, replaced by a loincloth and a crown of thorns. The silver tresses twisted into a matted veil of brown hair and oozing blood. The head tipped, the arms reached out as though to embrace the world. Nail marks blossomed in his palms; the wound from a spear point slashed across the side of his chest.

The dining room walls grew faintly transparent like frosted glass, and then vanished altogether. The transfigured body of Chi lifted off the ground to float suspended against a backdrop of thrashing trees and angry snow squalls. Spidery lightening flashed. Then flashed again. A basso voice drowned out the rolls of thunder, but couldn't keep the claps from pulsing through the floorboards beneath Kat's feet. Chi's lips never moved.

"THIS IS MY BELOVED SON, WITH WHOM I AM WELL PLEASED."

Jasper Thomas Petty fell to his knees, as much from fear as reverence. Rays of light flowered from around Chi's head, increasing in intensity until the young man was forced to cover his face with his hands. A whistle of wind climbed the scales, starting as a howl and becoming a screech. Only one thought filled Kat's head: "So this is what it's like to die."

Then silence.

Kat's eardrums throbbed and sweat dripped from his armpits. His hands trembled; his heart thudded in his chest. The silence was so complete, he could hear every lub and dub.

When the nothingness stretched from a handful of seconds to several minutes, he looked up.

Chi, wearing his rumpled black suit, sat smiling in the chair across from him. The table was set; the sandwich waiting; the candles flickering. The chandelier stretched its arms toward the ceiling again. The room had walls as solid as they had always been—before Kat had lost his mind.

"Cool, eh?"

Chi reached for another wedge of bologna sandwich. "Makes me hungry, though. Takes a lot out of a god, ya know?" He chewed thoughtfully for a moment, and then shook his head. "I don't know how Jose Perez did it night after night."

Kat slid his hands over the back of the chair where he'd been sitting—apparently for the entire time. It felt solid enough.

"Ever see *Steambath?*" Chi continued. "When it was on Broadway? It's a bit dated now but it was powerful stuff in its time. I tell you, when that towel boy, Morte, transformed himself into God Almighty, well... it took my breath away."

Kat stood slowly then swung his leg up and over the seat. He was being careful not to upset the chair, or his own teetering sanity. Stepping away from the table, he gazed at Chi with growing respect. "How'd you do that?"

Chi swallowed and dabbed at his lips with a corner of the tablecloth. "A magician never tells his secrets, my boy. Let's just say, you needed proof. I gave it to you." He motioned for Kat to finish the remaining half of sandwich. Then he scratched behind his ear and tried to look contrite. "I may have overshot a bit though. If so, I apologize. But, like I said, you are one stubborn mule. I figured it would take a big sales pitch to make you start listening."

"So you *are* God?"

Chi shook a warning finger. "Don't jump to conclusions." He pointed again at the sandwich. "Please, Kat. Sit. Eat. Listen. Only one explanation per customer, so keep your ears and mind open."

Kat shook his head, but did pick up the plate. "I think I'll stand, thanks." A small smile escaped onto his face. "Easier to dodge your next trick if I'm already on my feet, wouldn't you say?"

The man in the baggy black suit laughed and Kat took a big bite of his mother's peace offering. It tasted like a forkful of roast turkey topped with savory stuffing.

He didn't even notice.

D.L. Meyer & Valia Kapadai

Chapter 6

C hi raised his hands chest high, and made two fists. For a moment, Kat considered diving under the table. Then the man began to lift each finger in turn. "Alpha, beta, gamma, delta, epsilon," he intoned, "zêta, êta, thêta, iota, kappa." He clenched both hands again, and waited.

"Do I have to keep going?" he prompted.

Kat had forgotten to chew the last bite of his mother's sandwich. He swallowed it whole before answering. "It's the Greek alphabet."

"Bingo! And my name?"

The young man frowned and lowered the now-empty plate back to the table. There were twenty-four letters in the Greek alphabet. Kat had learned them all years ago just to win a bet with James.

"Yes, the women's sorority in *Revenge of the Nerds*," Chi acknowledged with a nod. "Jimbo didn't believe Lamda Mu were real Greek letters, did he? You sure showed him: memorized the damn thing overnight and collected five bucks for your trouble."

"How did you..." Kat started to ask. Then he closed his mouth with an audible smack.

Chi's grin grew wider.

Acceptance was short-lived. "Wait a minute!" Kat challenged, crossing to the other side of the table. "What are you trying to say here? That chi is part of the Greek alphabet? Because it isn't!"

"It most certainly is."

"No way. Uh-uh." Kat mouthed the rest of the letters to himself, but he knew he was right. He got as far as *tau, upsilon, phi,* when the skinny man interrupted.

"...*chi,* psi and omega."

"Key!" Kat corrected. An ah-ha was obvious in his voice. "It's pronounced key, not chi!"

The man tucked his chin to his chest and stared pointedly from under slitted lids. "Puhleeze, do not bicker with someone who has been around the block a couple million times or so."

"But it *is.*"

"Park your butt," Chi ordered. The chair Kat had vacated a few minutes before slid toward the two men like an exclamation point to his command. "Key is the way your physics teacher spoke Greek," he continued, waving Kat into the seat. "And *he* learned it from his fraternity. A Renaissance scholar named Erasmus popularized that pronunciation. To be precise, however, it's more like the 'ch' in Bach or loch. Very guttural and German—which is why I never favored it."

"But..."

"Shut it, kid. I'm on a roll."

Chi tilted back in his chair, one leg crossed, the ankle resting on his knee.

Kat's chair tipped back as well, startling him so much he nearly upended it.

"Whoa, careful, little buddy." The seat wobbled under Kat's butt, but achieved a comfortable balance. "Good. Now where was I? Oh yeah..."

The chandelier above them began to brighten, and the walls around them thinned. Only this time, the winter storm that raged outside was no longer visible. It had been replaced by an Elizabethan courtyard framed in marble arches. A stooped man in a ruby-colored doublet and purple stockings sat hunched to Kat's right.

"Jasper, meet the mastermind behind the first printed copies of the Greek New Testament!"

Doublet man shook his head and rattled off a string of incomprehensible syllables.

What? Kat puzzled. *I didn't understand a word of that.*

"Of course not," his new houseguest said in English. "It was all Greek to you."

Chi joined him in a fit of giggles. "All Greek to him," he agreed, slapping the table in glee. "All Greek to *everybody!*"

"Funny," Kat muttered. "A laugh riot."

The two men sobered, then rolled their eyes. "No sense of humor, Erasmus. Best just to get on with it."

The man nodded, pushed aside the empty china plate and folded his hands on the tabletop. "Ah, yes, the pronunciation of the Greek letter X. Well, *my* pronunciation is widespread among scholars, but it is actually very different from the way average Greeks pronounced it."

The soothing strains of a dulcimer rose beneath his words like the theme music to a bad history docudrama. A spangling of gold χ's drifted down around them, dancing like butterflies in a breeze. Kat put his head on the table and covered it with his arms. He couldn't shut out the music any more than he could muffle the moan that escaped his lips.

"Ignore him," Chi said. "I'm riveted. Go on."

Kat felt the table lurch as Erasmus rose to entertain his captive audience. The hem of his doublet hiked up briefly and Kat caught glimpse of a chubby bottom covered in velvet trunk-hose.

"Interestingly," the man continued in sonorous tones,

"modern Greek pronunciation is more closely similar to New Testament Greek than what your era would call Erasmian— but it is still not identical. There were many Greek dialects, and no single way to pronounce the letter X, even in my era."

The man took a deep breath, indicating he planned to continue. For Kat, it was sleep or swear time. "Okay, stop!" He lifted his head and hands skyward. "What does any of this have to do with the meaning of your name?"

"My name?" the scholar asked.

"My name," Chi corrected.

"X?"

"χ."

"Chi?"

"Key!" Kat yelled, leaping to his feet.

Both men fell silent.

"A bit dramatic, isn't he?" Erasmus observed.

"Puts Virgil to shame," Chi agreed. "Would you like to do the honors?"

The Renaissance scholar nodded. Gesturing palm up at the man in the black suit, he said simply: "I am pleased to introduce Χριστός. Or as you would say, the Christ."

Ah hah! That's what I did *say,* Kat gloated. *But he told me 'don't assume'.*

Chi shrugged an apology. "His words, not mine."

Before Kat could respond, the old scholar was off again. "In early versions of my New Testament," he droned, "the letter X—or chi—is the first letter of Christ. Of course, since the mid-sixteenth century, early Christians wishing to avoid persecution had begun to use it—or a similar Roman letter X—as an abbreviation for Christ…"

Kat threw up a finger to bookmark a stopping point in the lecture. His face relaxed into a smile. A woman's face slipped out of his memories.

On cue, Erasmus began to grow taller and thinner, stopping only when he had reached a lofty six-foot one-inch. His doublet lengthened into an ankle-length choir robe, his cheeks blossomed with rouge spots, and his hair retreated into a tight bun. Mrs. Clara Bandwell finished the story in her happy piping voice:

"…So as you can see, my dear children, Xmas is actually a perfectly acceptable abbreviation for Christmas."

Buried deep inside Kat's recollections, a seven-year-old Jasper grinned. Kat had forgotten how much he loved Mrs. Bandwell's stories. He wished he could tell her so now.

Chi sobered and uncrossed his legs. "She's glad to hear it."

The woman beamed and patted Kat's cheek, but she faded before he could revel in her touch. The marble arches faded with her, along with the dining room table. Grandma Iris's lost inheritance vanished too. And then the house. Chi stood up just as the chair on which he'd been holding court dissolved into a whisper of ice crystals.

"I didn't lead you astray, Kat. You needed a name—a reality to cling to. For you, a Christ figure worked best. But I am you. And I am more than you. I am what you could be if you would let yourself live as fully as life allows."

Chi held out his palm. After a moment's hesitation, the young man took hold of it.

"People in the Orient would tell you chi is a life-force—and they would be correct."

Kat felt his feet lift off the floor. The crystals that had once been a chair spun themselves into a spiral to surround them, catching at Kat's shirt, the hem of his pants, the hair on his head. In seconds, it carried them above the rooftops, the tree tops, and the cloud tops beyond.

"For unlettered folks, chi is an X that can be used to make your mark when you've never been given enough schooling to write your own name. And they would be right too."

Kat should have been terrified, but his quotient for terror had been surpassed long before this. The sight of the stars flickering above the storm and the glow of the sun disappearing over the curve of the world were just part and parcel of the night's insanity. It hadn't killed him yet and he suspected now it never would.

Chi pointed away from the setting sun toward many small clusters of city lights, dotting the landscape here and there, bending away from them to the east—a necklace of communities leading them onward.

Personally, Chi thought to Kat. *I like to think of myself as the X on a treasure map.* The man twisted his wrist and the swirl of crystals turned with it, darting forward like an arrow toward the unknown. *Let us see where it lies for you, Jasper Thomas Petty.*

D.L. Meyer & Valia Kapadai

Chapter 7

Up here, wrapped in darkness, with the stars and planets so sharp and close, Kat became aware of just how fragile he was. How insignificant. How alone. If Chi let go of his hand, he would plunge through the atmosphere to become a bloody stain on someone's lawn. Just another life that came and went. His problems unresolved. His desires unrequited.

Would anyone care? Should *they care? We come into the world alone. We leave it alone.*

"So much still to learn, Jasper." Chi shook his head and the silver locks that had been streaming behind him flared briefly into a cloud. "Being alone is an unnatural state. It takes work—and you've been putting in a lot of overtime."

But I date.

"Forget the Caroles. They're a smoke screen. You choose them on purpose because they *are* Caroles. It's safer that way."

The spangle of lights beneath them tipped upward suddenly. Kat's hold tightened. Chi tucked his arm to his side, pulling the young man close. Kat's fear of falling eased; his discomfort at the intimate contact skyrocketed.

"Kat, Kat, Kat," Chi scolded. "Being alone is greedy. It's selfish. It's stubborn. To remain alone an entire lifetime, a person has to keep himself wholly *to* himself." Without relinquishing his grip, Chi slipped his arm around Kat's waist, bending Kat's elbow into the small of his back. "Give in, give back, and doh-see-doh. Life is a dance, kid. It requires partners."

The lights beneath them stopped being pinpricks. Some grew to a recognizable size, pairing off and racing along narrow paths that branched right and left; glowing white on the cars that moved toward them; winking red on the vehicles pulling away. Other lights remained stationary, becoming illuminated blocks of houses, factories and high-rises. One jagged mountain range of structures loomed ahead, growing stronger and brighter as they approached. "Columbia, South Carolina," Chi called out loudly. "All ashore who's going ashore." The men overshot the city's center, skimming a glittering array of office buildings. A sidewalk climbed to meet them. They slowed.

Three feet from the ground, Chi let go of Kat's hand. The young man fell. His feet touched terra firma first and he stumbled. His legs gave way. He toppled hard onto his knees.

"Alone sucks, don't it?" Chi observed.

Kat leapt up and dusted a few dried leaves from his pants. Then he turned his back on the smug face. He wouldn't give the man the satisfaction of seeing him bruise.

This place was far different from Chugwater. The first thing Kat noticed was the air, uncomfortably warm and humid. The second was the dreariness. No upscale neighborhood here. The houses were narrow and sandwiched side-by-side; hardly any lawns to speak of, and few Christmas lights. One streetlamp burned at the corner, illuminating a smattering of cars lining the curb. All of them were black or nearly so. All of them were broad and heavy. All of them were humped like buffalo. These looked nothing like the candy-colored vehicles Kat was used to seeing in the parking lot at TF&F. These cars were...

"Old," Chi confirmed. "Approximately 1955 old."

"Christmas past."

"No, actually, Christmas future. Your future." Chi set off for the nearest house, a clapboard dwelling with a sagging stoop. A candle stub burned in the window. A rough circlet of balsam branches tried hard to adorn the door. The silver-haired man looked back once before climbing the steps. "Come see. The sooner you learn, the sooner we can both go home to bed."

The door opened directly onto a living room. A man and a woman sat cross-legged on the floor surrounded by boxes. The container closest to Kat was the size of a small filing cabinet and was lettered in red grease pencil.

"Kitchen Stuff," he read.

He didn't realize immediately that he had spoken out loud but the couple did not react. Now that he thought about it, they hadn't looked up when Chi opened the door either.

"Oh come on, you know the drill. They can't hear us. They can't see us. They are the lesson. You are the dunce in the corner."

The room was barely large enough for the couple and their packed possessions. A brass lamp minus its shade huddled in the corner throwing harsh beams of light up the bare walls. A door stood open at the far back of the room. Beyond it in the dark Kat could just make out the shadowy bulk of an old-fashioned ice box. A narrow archway to the right was hung with dark green fabric sprouting large magenta roses. The last time Kat had seen a pattern like it had been on his Great Grandma Petty's overstuffed sofa. The only other item in the room, besides the couple and the boxes, was a miniscule Christmas tree, draped in a handmade newspaper chain and propped on top of an upturned crate against the left-hand wall. Sawed-off stumps around its trunk indicated this was the source of the branches that had been tied together to make a wreath for the home's front door.

The man grasped a large box with both hands and wiggled it back and forth until he had walked it to a point midway between himself and the woman. "Heavy, Esther," he groaned. "What's in this one?" Picking up a penknife, he inserted it into the gap where the top and the sidewalls met.

"Be careful, Jack!" she shouted. "Those are my books."

The man halted his movements. The woman clapped a hand over her mouth. Both turned toward the curtained doorway and listened. Several heartbeats later, they slumped in relief.

"Sorry," she added more softly. "I keep forgetting how close he is here."

"It's okay. He didn't wake up. Crisis averted." The man put the knife back on the floor and reached across the box to cup her cheek. "It's all going to work out. You know that don't you? This is only temporary."

The woman covered his fingers with hers. "I know. It's just…" Her lower lip trembled. "So much has happened… so close together… so near to the holiday…"

In the room's harsh light, Kat saw her eyes shine with unshed tears.

"No presents… his first Christmas… I tried to make a stocking… I thought I could bake him a cookie to hide inside it… from the last of our flour and sugar, you know? But it took all of that ugly chintz just to make coverings for the bedroom door. Not enough for anything else. The stocking ended up looking like a lumpy mitten." The tears brimmed and, despite her best efforts, slipped down one cheek to her chin. Their clasped hands caught and held the other tears at bay.

"Esther, Esther," the man soothed, leaning forward to

comfort his wife. "He'll never remember this. Next year, I'll have found a new job. Mom will help keep us afloat until then. We'll pay her back. We'll buy presents…" The box was too large a barrier to his solace. Unwinding his legs, he crawled on his knees to her side. His hand never left her face.

Esther's hold on him was so intense Kat doubted Jack could have released her even if he had wanted to.

"We'll buy the biggest tree we can find, and load it with so many ornaments I'll have to tie it to nails in the wall to hold it up!"

His wife was sobbing now, though softly so as not to wake the baby.

He settled back on his haunches in front of her. His free hand cupped the other side of her face and tipped it up till their eyes met. "And a turkey. A thirty-pounder. With all the trimmings. We'll invite your mom."

Esther's sobs grew a smidgen louder.

"She can bring pasta."

"Pasta?" she hiccupped.

"Uh-huh," he soothed. "A big pot. You love pasta. Noel has your strong Italian streak. He will love it too."

Their son's name must have reached beyond the magenta roses and alerted the baby that he was the subject of discussion. A feeble whine called in answer.

"Shh," the wife hushed her husband, her voice a tremulous mixture of giggles and tears. "We'll never get done if he wakes up again."

The father of her baby chuckled in return, and then pressed his mouth to hers. The room grew quiet. Baby Noel followed suit.

After a moment, the couple parted.

"My Jack," the wife sighed. "My great strong Jack. What would I do without you?"

The man rose to his feet and crossed behind her, taking her hand with him. He resettled himself on the patch of floor at her back then pulled her against his chest. Her captured fingers found a home next to his cheek. His other arm wrapped around her waist to protect her from the world. She buried her nose in his shirt sleeve and inhaled his scent.

"We should at least finish the living room," she whispered.

"Leave it for morning," he murmured in her ear. "We'll pretend the boxes are presents and everything inside them is new."

Her giggle was stronger this time as she lifted her head to tuck it under his chin. Stacked like faces on a totem pole, they gazed past Chi and Kat to the pitiful tree on its makeshift table. The newspaper chain fluttered. Small wisps of breath escaped the woman's parted lips. The room had a draft that Kat could not feel. The husband and wife were oblivious to it as well. They were at peace.

Kat couldn't resist moving closer to study their faces. He and Esther spoke in unison. "What if next year is the same as this year?"

Kat bent over to look into Jacks' eyes. *He knows already. He's down on his luck—this time maybe for the count.*

"By this time next year," he asked Chi, "one or both of them will have thrown in the towel, right?"

"Think so?" the man in black asked. "Watch and learn."

Jack tightened his hold on his wife and his eyes glowed. "Then I will be the luckiest man on earth," he answered her. "I will still have you and Noel."

Esther smiled. She shifted in his arms to shake a finger in his face. "Just promise me one thing, Jack McShirin."

"What, my feisty one?"

"Whatever else happens, promise me six yards of good blue fabric to replace those awful cheap roses."

The two young people laughed softly but the merriment didn't last long. Esther fingered the button on the cuff of Jack's shirt then slipped it from its mooring. With a deep sigh, she slid her hand inside his sleeve to fondle the flesh of his muscled arm.

The newspaper chain on the tree fluttered again, and as the couple stretched out amidst the boxes of their pretend Christmas, a red light flickered among the headlines. Then a blue light. And then a green. Soon dozens of lights joined them, illuminating the silver and red glass balls that grew from the tree's branches. A gold star sprouted from the top. Strings of tinsel drifted down its flanks. The box disappeared beneath a snowy sheet.

Jack and Esther saw none of it. They were lost in each other's warmth, mouths searching for and finding all they needed to make their holiday whole.

"Next year," Chi said. "They will still be here. They will still be struggling. They will still be happy."

Kat looked at him, and frowned. "How? How can they do it? Take blow after blow and pretend it doesn't matter?"

Chi took Kat's hand and the house faded around them. The answer he gave seemed no answer at all.

"Great Grandma Iris sold all her possessions of value. Jack and Esther will hold on to theirs."

Chapter 8

Jasper Petty had no problem identifying their next destination. What did startle him was the image of the twin towers silhouetted against a full moon.

"Almost didn't get out of bed that morning," Chi said as they skirted the heart-stopping buildings. "Wasn't sure I could bear all those desperate prayers. Those whispered good-byes."

Kat twisted his head as they passed, his eyes lingering on the lighted windows and the tiny scurrying figures within. How many of the people he was seeing now would be there on that future day?

"A lot of them," Chi responded. "But some will be lucky. Their loved ones will be on the other end of the line when they call. Too many others will speak their heart to the impersonal ear of an answering machine."

The towers drifted behind them, becoming tangled in the New York skyline. Kat pulled his gaze away.

"Why?" he asked.

"Why it happened?"

"Why you let it happen."

Chi would not look at him but Kat thought he saw pain in the hardening of the man's jaw. "Mankind creates its own hells," he answered, pointing to the streets below.

They were descending again and Kat tried to see what the man meant. At first, he noted only the inching traffic and the yellow taxis jockeying for win, place and show. But as they drew nearer, other details emerged: a woman screaming and flailing her arms at a man whose bumper was mangled against hers; a street gang taunting a pair of tourists; a doorman shooing a homeless man off the steps of a high-toned brownstone.

"Of course," Chi added, "they create their own heavens too."

Kat could see no heaven below but he figured he would soon enough. He was becoming resigned to the fact that another lesson was just around the corner—or the next skyscraper.

In this case it was at 254 West 54th Street in Manhattan.

The two men stepped down just outside the doors of Studio 54 where a line of wannabe patrons stood herded together behind velvet ropes stretching down the block. "Look. There's Steve Rubell," Chi indicated with a tip of his head. A flamboyantly attired man was just stepping out of the club to survey the crowd. "He's one of the partners and the gatekeeper here. Watch everyone try to catch his eye, without catching his eye, if you get what I mean."

Kat turned to look back at the beautiful people lining 54th Street, and was agog at the number of celebrities mixing with the pretty nobodies. Each of them was younger and fresher than they would be thirty years hence: Donald Trump, Sly Stallone, Sir Elton John...

"He's not a sir yet," Chi corrected.

The glitterati also included a posing Liza Minnelli and a radiant Liz Taylor. Brooke Shields decorated the arm of Michael Jackson, but neither of them seemed confident about getting in. Bette Midler was easy to spot—and hear, as she shrieked hello to a fellow celeb. The surprise in the line was Lillian Carter.

"Some of these folks are long gone now," Chi said. "It's kind of fun to see them again."

When Kat looked confused, the man wrapped an arm around his shoulders and gave him a squeeze. "Not everyone ends up in my neighborhood when they die, Jasper. It's best not to forget that."

Studio 54's Steve Rubell lowered the velvet barrier and waved a few of his chosen ones inside. Among them were the late Andy Warhol, Truman Capote and Freddie Mercury.

"Mick and Bianca are already dancing on the moon," Chi said cryptically. "Let's join them, shall we?"

Chapter 9

The floor vibrated under the weight of gyrating bodies. So many, at first Kat didn't see what Chi had been referring to. Then a cherry-red painting of the man in the moon appeared beneath the dancers' feet. Kat squinted through the forest of legs and frowned at the weary-looking face adorning the floor—and at the coke spoon teasing its nose. *Does he really look weary? Or is that only in hindsight?*

"Take a good gander, Kat," Chi shouted over the thrum of disco music blasting from the club's formidable sound system. "These are the world's movers and shakers in 1978."

Kat rolled his eyes. "Another knee-slapper, Chi?"

"What?"

A deafening wha-wha bass track had swallowed his words and he had to repeat them ten decibels louder to be heard.

"I said, 'Another knee-slapper?'"

"What??" Chi shouted again. "A mean rapper? Wrong era, kid."

"Not 'mean rapper'. Knee-slapper! Movers and shakers... on a dance floor... moving and shaking..."

Chi scrunched up his forehead and frowned. "Sorry, kid. I don't get it."

An emaciated man dressed in purple silk and sporting silver-lamé platform boots stepped in front of Kat, smiling broadly.

"First time at the Studio?" he asked. "There's a great view from the balconies, sweetheart. Would you like me to show you?" A wink and a once-over from his heavily painted eyes hinted the man had something more in mind.

Kat curled the fingers of his right hand into a fist, and cocked his elbow. A woman's voice, cool and sassy, spoke up from behind, stopping Kat from introducing lamé boy's chin to his hard Wyoming knuckles.

"Pardonnez-moi, Monsieur, mais vous m'avez confondu pour un flétan."

The man rocked back on his heels, and raised a pair of penciled-in eyebrows so high they became buried in his hairline. "Whoa, a French dolly!"

He pinched a dab of suspicious white powder from his nose, and stretched out his arm between Chi and Kat. "Whatever you said, mademoiselle, I couldn't agree more. Take my arm—for now. We can talk about the rest of me later."

Kat turned to see the woman's reaction. He was startled to note she was dressed in jeans and an off-the-shoulder white sweater. *Rather plain attire for Studio 54.*

"She doesn't need flash to shine," Chi pointed out.

Kat had to agree. The woman was standing next to an attractive friend, but it took a moment before anyone noticed that. The first female was a skyrocket; the second—though pretty—was a wisp of trailing smoke.

He studied her features with interest. She wasn't conventionally lovely. Her forehead was high and her nose long. And when she frowned as she was doing now, her chin had a stubborn hardness. But her hair was shiny auburn, brushing the top of her bare shoulder as she cocked her head and looked confused. *And her eyes,* Kat extolled. *Brown as sable, and twice as soft.*

"Take my arm," glam man coaxed.

When the woman made no move to accept his offer, he shouted at the top of his lungs. "Take my arm, baby! My arm."

The music slammed to a stop and for a brief respite there was silence. Her answer filled it nicely.

"Okay, but what do I do once I've got it? Looks to me like your scrawny ass can't spare a single limb."

Peals of laughter rose like sharks to blood. Fortunately for the man, the next wave of music drowned out the jeers. He flipped the young woman the bird, then slipped away as gracefully as his high heels would allow.

The not-so-French dolly leaned in to whisper in her friend's ear. Despite the noise, Kat could hear her easily.

"Balcony? With him? Right."

"Do you think it's true, Ginie?" her friend asked. "That people have sex up there?" She pointed with her chin at the balconies overhanging the dance floor.

"No time like the present to find out."

Ginie grabbed the girl's elbow to steer her towards a set of stairs. The friend pulled away.

"Are you nuts?"

"Aw, Beth, don't be a wet blanket. We came here to mingle with the hedonists, didn't we? To experience what Oscar Wilde would have called 'the only real colour-element left in modern life'? Well this is it, Bethie. Sin. So experience, already!"

Beth hesitated, her eyes wary. When she smiled, it became obvious her features weren't just pretty; they were far better put together than those of her bold friend. Still, Ginie was the prize here and Kat wished he could meet her in her own time and place.

"To sleep, perhaps to dream," Chi yelled to him over Sly

and the Family Stone.

"Enough with the Oscar Wilde crap, Ginie. At least ninety percent of the ghouls here wouldn't even recognize the name." Beth stood on tiptoe to peer over her friend's shoulder. "I wager there isn't even one God-fearing male with a brain in the entire bunch. I can't imagine why you wanted to come here."

Ginie turned to survey the dance floor. Though she couldn't see him, she stared directly into Kat's eyes. "We are *all* in the gutter, Bethie," she murmured, knowing her friend couldn't possibly hear her. "But some of us are looking at the stars."

Beth craned her neck to try and catch the words. "You did it again, didn't you? Another Oscarism? You quoted him again! You are hopeless, girl."

Ginie linked her arm in Beth's and grinned. Then she headed them toward a bank of tables. "I can switch to Wilfred Owen," she teased. "Or how about some lyrics from Claude Francois?"

"How about a whiskey sour and a pair of ear plugs."

"The music is loud in here, isn't it?" Ginie agreed.

"I meant *you.*"

Several minutes of elbowing and excuse-me's yielded mixed results. The young women discovered it was quieter in the more sheltered back areas of the club, but dozens of other patrons had beat them to it. There were no empty tables.

Beth fretted; Ginie saw it as an opportunity to explore the nether regions of Studio 54. "Come on, Bethie. Who knows what kinds of vice exist behind the scenes. We'll just look, not touch. Debauchery is only mildly contagious, you know. I promise I'll throw myself over your body if I think there's even the slightest chance you'll catch something."

Kat and Chi saw it first, but Ginie was equally sharp. A man standing nearby had lifted a beer to his lips to hide a grin.

Ginie's eyes sparked like flint. "Eavesdropping?" she asked.

Faking surprise, the young man glanced left then right, before pointing to his chest with the bottle. "Me?"

"Mmmm," she answered with a curt nod.

He grinned again, this time without the beer to shield him. "Shamelessly."

"That isn't very polite."

"True. A real gentleman would have ignored you completely." He sipped his beer and let his eyes roam over her face. "A man with a decorous upbringing would have noticed immediately that despite your obvious pulchritude you are an individual of the highest moral rectitude, an unassailable Puritan, a pinnacle of propriety..."

"Huh?" Beth grunted. "What was that? Earth-speak please."

Ginie poked her in the ribs. Her eyes crinkled at the corners. "Yes? Go on."

"I of course am an alien to these environs," he continued, his eyes answering hers crinkle for crinkle. "So I do not qualify. I am only a quasi-gentleman. I admit I have followed your movements from the very moment you stepped through those doors." He lifted his brown bottle to her in a toast before finishing his thought. "And while other more depraved males may have thought otherwise, I most certainly did not mistake you for a halibut."

Kat scratched his head and turned to Chi in confusion. Ginie's sable eyes widened and her mouth dropped open to emit a bray-like laugh, followed by a delighted snort.

"Mmm," the man said with a smile. "Very ladylike."

"You speak French!" she blurted amidst a flurry of giggles. "Beth, he speaks French."

Beth rolled her eyes and searched for somewhere to hide. Ginie's laughter had drawn a lot of unwanted attention. "He speaks more than *that*. He's all yours. I'm going in search of that sour."

Neither the man nor Ginie noticed her departure.

"So what are two marginally literate individuals like us doing in Studio 54?" the man asked. "You first."

Ginie shrugged and her sweater dipped lower on her bare shoulder. "Me? I am a daredevil. Stunts like this keep my blood pumping. Beth is my conscience. She keeps me honest—and my head on straight." Her eyes left his only long enough to pan the room. "I mean how can you be young and alive in 1978 and *not* see this? There's more to getting an education than taking classes and chasing a degree."

"So you're a student then?"

"Columbia," she acknowledged. "English literature."

"Really? Me too. I mean a Columbia student. Or at least I was. I finally nailed an MBA last quarter. Doing time in the financial district right now, before looking for less cold-blooded employment in the heartland." Another smile lit his face and Kat began to grow jealous. This was the kind of guy he hated most: accomplished, confident and erudite.

"Everything you wanted to be," Chi pointed out. "But abandoned in favor of... what, Kat?"

Survival, he thought with anger. *For my mom. I had no choice.*

Ginie's brows pulled together. "Afraid of failing in Gotham, Mr. Quasi-gentleman?"

The man's eyebrows arched upward. "Quite the opposite, Miss Halibut. Afraid of succeeding."

When her face relaxed, Kat knew it was the answer she had been angling for. The young man did too. He lifted a hand to the side of her face and tucked her hair behind her ear. "I bet you are the kind of woman who argues when a man tells her she's beautiful."

For the first time since hearing her voice, Kat realized Ginie was speechless. The best she could manage was a single strong nod.

"Too bad," her young man said. "Then I guess we'll be arguing about it for—say—the next sixty or seventy years." He lowered his arm and extended his hand. "My name's Noel. What's yours?"

Chapter *10*

K at wanted one more minute to fall deeper into Ginie's eyes; just sixty more seconds to envy Jack and Esther's baby boy, now grown. But the walls were fading around him, snatching *Lady Marmalade*, Mick Jagger and a cokehead moon back into the past. He curled his toes in a futile attempt to grab hold of this decade and make it his own. But it was no use. Everything vanished.

"No! I wasn't ready. I don't know what I am supposed to learn from this. Go back."

Chi didn't answer.

A bone-shattering cold seeped through Kat's pores. His head spun and his pulse raced.

I'm going to pass out. What's going on?

There was no answering thought.

A stiff wind whipped at Kat's shirt, threatening to tear it from his arms. Chi must be moving at light speed toward some other far-off city. Kat forced his eyes open as wide as they would go, but he could pick out no glittering buildings in the void below. No streets. No dark bulk of mountains against the gray curvature of Earth. He could see nothing at all.

Wait. There. What's that?

A patch of brown. Rough. Barren. Like a long flat prairie. Were they moving north? West? Maybe home?

"What is that? Where are we going?" he called out in the dark. Chi only whistled in return, a high quavering note that he held forever. Something wasn't right. The air felt different. Violent. It stung Kat's cheeks, and hurt his head—the very front part of his head, just above his eyebrow. He shifted his gaze to where Chi should have been clasping his hand, hurtling him through space.

The man wasn't there. Kat's sight was unimpeded all the way to the distant line of demarcation between the naked prairie and...

Nothing.

The patch of brown simply stopped. Beyond it, only flat white ground. The line between the two plains was strange too. It was straight as a razor cut. Straight as the line you draw in the dirt before giving a double-dog dare. Straight as a knife edge that only the bravest would challenge.

Chi whistled again, raising gooseflesh on Kat's arms and the back of his neck.

"Where the hell are you?" Kat hollered, twisting his neck to the left and over his shoulder.

A puff of icy crystals stung his eyes. A smell of damp cloth filled his nostrils. A row of white wooden slats stood guard across the horizon. Slats like those on the railing of his mother's front porch.

"Wha...?"

Jasper Petty swung his gaze forward, searching for landmarks. Arching his back, he could make out black shadows painting the dead brown landscape below, shadows that looked strangely like words.

Merry Christmas

A key ring lay near the message, dotting the i.

"Chi!" he yelled, lurching to one knee. A drift of snow cascaded off his shoulder and down the front of his old jacket. His head yelled back, crying out with a pain so sharp it nearly sent him tumbling back to the porch floor—a pain centered on a spot just above his left eyebrow.

How long have I been lying here? Did I fall? "Mom!" he shouted.

His head reminded him not to do that again.

Scrabbling for his keys, Kat snatched at the door handle and levered himself to his feet. It took a moment for his body to stop swaying. The wind at his back did nothing to help. Once steady, he fingered through the choices on the ring until he found the brass one with the sharp tip.

Kat hunched over to get a better look at the three keyholes swimming before him. He was about to go for hole number two when he halted. Was the insane evening going to start all over again? For a moment, he closed his eyes; then, in one quick motion, he jerked his head upright. The door window glowed with the warm light from within. No one frowned out through its frosty pane.

"Thank God!" he cried, forgetting the warning from the knot on his head.

With shaking fingers, Kat succeeded in pushing the key into the lock and giving it a twist. The tumblers clicked and the doorknob turned. His mother's tiny vestibule yawned before him. Warm. Quiet. Empty. He stumbled inside, sliding on unsteady legs.

"Mom?"

The kitchen at the end of the hall was in shadow. The dining room door was closed. The parlor to his right was lit, but dimly. Great Grandma Petty's ruby-glass lamp was dark.

This was the house he had returned to at evening's end every day of his adult life. Safe and unchanged. No quirky guests. No unsettling questions. No mind-altering surprises.

Kat removed his jacket, sending drifts of snow-melt splattering across the tile floor. Should he hang it in the guest closet, or run it upstairs? A memory of Lakshmi rose before him, her eight arms beckoning to help.

"How the hell did I dream *that* up?" he mumbled to himself. If the entire evening had been a hallucination, then the images that appeared to him should have risen from his subconscious. Kat couldn't recall ever reading about the Hindu goddess Lakshmi. Or the sun god Sol Invictus. Or Mithras. Or even much about Boxing Day. Kat shook his head, sending shockwaves of pain shooting out from his forehead to both temples.

"Too much Discovery Channel," he decided, tossing his wet coat onto the floor.

He turned right, into the parlor, and stopped. His mother had decorated for the holidays: A tree stood in the front window. Candles and holly festooned the mantle. Two needlework pillows adorned the red velvet settee, each depicting a holiday scene. One featured a man in a black suit wearing red socks and a red scarf, his arms and mouth stretched wide as he sang a carol on a snowy street.

These were the things the woman had done every December since her husband died. Exactly the same. As though going through the motions would bring back the magic. Would bring back the man. Despite his mother's attempts to make the room festive, Kat felt nothing here but despair.

Defying the ache in his head, Kat rushed to the ruby lamp and snapped it on. Then he dashed to the tree, fumbled for the plug on the floor and jammed it into a socket. Righting himself, he stared about with panicked eyes. The colored lights only heightened the feeling of anguish. He could start a fire, even put on some Christmas music, but it wouldn't change the fact that he was alone here. Or relieve the guilt of knowing his mother had been alone here too for sixteen years.

No wonder she had rushed off to be with Mark. The Charlie Brown tree in Jack and Esther's barren living room had been far merrier than this. They had had each other. Their happiness during even the most dismal of Christmas seasons had not been dependant on elaborate decorations or angels singing in the walls.

"Did she go to Mark?"

Abandoning the decked-out parlor, Kat moved toward the hall and the shuttered dining room door.

"Mom?"

He heard nothing but she responded just the same. Her sandwich waited on the table, a square of white paper tucked under the edge of the plate. There was no lace-edged table linen or silver-rimmed china. Grandma Iris could keep them, as far as Kat was concerned. His mom's homey blue plastic plate and jelly-jar glass were a banquet to be savored with his eyes and heart.

> *Hello darling…*
>
> *I hope you had fun with Jim and Lolita. I'm sorry I won't be here to listen to your clever stories about their first pregnancy. Mark asked me to dinner. Will try to call you later. All my love,*
>
> *Mom.*
>
> *PS- Sweet dreams.*

"The sweetest to you too, Mom," he murmured.

He was surprised to realize he wasn't a bit upset. The thought of his mother finding a new way to celebrate life brought a smile to his face. But the smile faltered a second later as he realized what the letter really meant.

"Chi was real!"

How could Kat have known this snack would be waiting for him? How could he have known his mother would be going to Mark's for dinner? If he had truly fallen and hit his head, he could not have been inside the house to see it.

He picked up a wedge of the sandwich—cut into quarters as she had not done in many years. White bread. Bologna. Tomato. With mayo. The proof couldn't have been stronger if he'd found half the snack missing and a pile of telltale crumbs in its place.

Still, he should call Mark to make sure. The storm was whistling Chi's chilling tune outside the windows: a long high quavering wail. If his mother had gone out on her own, she could be trapped somewhere needing his help.

The phone called for him instead.

He dropped the sandwich and dashed to the kitchen. "Mom?" he hollered into the receiver, expecting a buzz of static. Silence filled the line for many heartbeats. When a voice finally responded it was not Evelyn Petty.

"Kat?" a man spoke softly. "Jasper?"

"Yeah," he answered in surprise. "Jim? Is that you? Wow, I didn't recognize you for a second there. Yeah. It's me. Sorry, I thought my mom was calling. I…"

"Kat?"

"Yeah." This time his voice matched the softness of his friend's tone.

James's sigh reached through the line and grabbed his throat. "Can you come, Kat?"

It never occurred to him to ask why. His friend's pain was loud and clear. "Yes. Sure. I'm leaving now."

"I know the weather is rotten. Maybe…"

"I'm leaving now, Jim. Where am I going? Where are you?"

A second sigh ripped through the line. "The hospital."

Jim said nothing more and Kat nearly hung up, already planning how to get the truck out of the garage and past the drifts that would block the driveway at the bottom of the hill.

Then his friend spoke again.

"The baby is early, Kat. There's blood. A lot of blood."

"I'm coming, Jim. I'm hanging up right now and I'm coming." Then he added a lie, because he knew a lie was called for. "It's going to be all right."

"I don't know," Jim said slowly. Kat could almost see his friend's large body sagging against a wall, his big hands strangling a tiny cell phone. A sob erupted from the earpiece. And then another. "I don't think so, Kat. I really, really don't think so."

Chapter *11*

S on of a bitch!"

Kat threw the truck into drive and felt it lurch forward against the great pile of snow. *How in the hell did it get so deep so quickly?* He had slammed into the three-foot drift at least five times already, but had done nothing more than create an imprint of the vehicle's grill in the wall of white.

"It's not going to happen," he groaned. He was never going to get to Jim. He was never going to get out of his own driveway. Still, he had to keep trying. He zigzagged the gearshift into reverse. Then with one foot on the brake and the other crushing the accelerator, he revved the engine as high as it could handle. When he popped the brake, the truck flew backwards, slewing in the icy tracks behind him. He spun the wheel, and the truck corrected its spin. But then wallowed too far to the left. With a sickening whoof, he felt the back tires slide off the driveway and into the drainage ditch. A black patch of roiling clouds now filled the windshield. Kat could no longer see the snow drift or the road beyond—only an angry sky.

He dropped his head unto the steering wheel, triggering a stab of pain from the bruise above his left eye. He had lied to Jim twice tonight. He wouldn't be coming after all.

"No," he cried, wrenching himself upright. "I walked home; I can walk to the hospital."

He was being an ass and he knew it. The weather was giving the orders. Any fool who defied them deserved to die frozen to the tarmac.

He unlatched his seatbelt, and pulled on the door handle. A scream of wind pushed back as he shoved his way out. He was rewarded for his efforts with a fast slide down the icy embankment and a hard landing on his left knee. He stood up quickly, pulling the back of his jacket away from his waist. Snow had rammed itself under the nylon and up his spine. Jerking his shoulders, he tried vainly to knock it free. What did fall out sifted into his jeans and the tops of his boots.

From where he stood, Kat could see the street lights lining the road just beyond the drift. If he turned one-eighty, he would see the tracks of truck tires leading back to the house. Either way would be brutal, but success was more likely if he climbed the driveway instead of the drift.

"There's blood. A lot of blood."

"But there's nothing I can do about it. They're at the hospital where there are doctors and nurses. What good will it do Jim if I kill myself trying to get to him?" The wind shoved him in the back. It was a warning to heed the truth in his words. A whiteout could cause him to lose his way. A slip down another ravine could knock him out and leave him to be buried by the heavy snow. The wind chill alone could make him hypothermic and shut down his organs before he reached his destination.

"Go home, Kat. Call the hospital and tell Jim you'll get there as soon as you can tomorrow."

He nodded to himself twice, and looked back over his shoulder at the Christmas lights winking at him through the parlor window.

Kat Petty reached up and slammed the truck door. Then he climbed the drift.

Chapter *12*

It was even worse than he had feared. The blowing snow erased the margins alongside the roadway and filled hollows until they appeared flat and solid. More than once, he wandered onto the berm without noticing, tripping on hidden rocks and heel-sledding into potholes. The wind burned his eyes, even with the collar of his jacket pulled up around his ears. Eventually, he made it to the outskirts of town where High Street intersected State Route 25. The hospital was at least two miles farther out, but perhaps now he would have the luxury of treading on a plowed surface.

No such luck. Any work that road crews may have done—if they had been this way at all—had been wiped out by the high winds. Quitting was no longer an option, though. Kat had to keep walking. To stop would be suicide.

He heard the squeal and crunch of tires on hard-packed snow long before he saw any headlights. Turning his back to the wind, he watched for the vehicle's approach behind him. A tow truck sporting a red plow emerged from the darkness, tossing a rooster tail of white into the air and onto his side of the road. He gestured frantically, his hands crisscrossing above his head. The plow rose and the truck slowed, coming to a stop at his side. "Middletowne Auto & Truck Repair" was emblazoned in green on the door. The driver's window inched down a crack.

"Good lord! What are you doing out here? Get in before someone accidentally plows you under."

Kat gave a grateful thumbs-up and jogged around the front of the truck, the heat from its engine a welcoming warmth. The passenger-side door opened and he grabbed the frame to heave himself inside. "Thanks, buddy," he said, slamming the door behind him. "You have no idea how great it is to see you."

He turned to add a smile, but then froze.

The driver was a woman.

And not just any woman.

Ginie.

"I have an active imagination," she said with a grin that warmed him even more than the truck's heater. "I must look like a winning lottery ticket to you right about now!"

Like a million tickets, he was tempted to add. Then he remembered Jim.

"I need to get to the hospital," he said abruptly. "Can you take me there?"

She instantly sobered. "Sure thing. I should have known it was some sort of emergency."

The woman jerked the lever on the steering column to lower the plow, and then shifted the truck into drive. She glanced over at him once, as though waiting for a further explanation. When Kat remained silent, she turned her attention back to the road.

This cannot be Ginie, he insisted to himself. She wasn't the correct age. The real Ginie, if she had ever existed, would be nearly thirty years older than the woman at his side. Ginie would be a professor of English literature somewhere. Ginie would be cultured. Ginie would be successful, bright and wondrous. *This woman drives a truck, for heaven's sake. Probably has no more than a high school education.* Okay, yes, she did have the same kind of ethereal looks that could take your breath away. But a tow truck driver? A mechanic? A blue-collar laborer? What was that all about?

"I'm Carole Tamara McShirin from Upper Middletowne," she said, confirming she was no Ginie. "But everyone calls me Tam. And you are…?"

"Kat Petty from Chugwater. Jasper Petty, actually. But only the very brave, the very foolish, and my mother call me that."

"Hmm," she answered, leaning forward to scratch a crust of frost off the bottom corner of the windshield. "Cat with a C, like on a hot tin roof? Or Kat with a K, like in Katmandu?"

He smiled despite himself. "Neither," he corrected. "With a K, but like in Katarthis." He hesitated to go on. He didn't know her well enough to trust her with his lost dreams.

She gave him a quick look then refocused on the dangerous roadway. "That must be something else you would rather not share, hmm?"

Perceptive, he thought. And no derision in her tone. "I'm not sure there's enough time. Or enough language," he said.

"You don't have to explain. I'm just naturally nosey. Feel free to tell me to bug off."

He remained silent on the subject but was loathe to end the conversation. "Nosey is okay, as long as not answering is too."

She smiled and the truck's cab grew even warmer. "Of course. Je suis pas mal. Vous êtes l'homme pas mal, élégant."

His mind flashed on a sassy dolly in a New York disco and he responded without thinking. "You speak French! I would never have guessed!"

Tam's smile dimmed. She leaned forward and scratched at the windshield again, but this time the frost was in her reply. "And why is that, Kat-with-a-K? Did I strike you as someone with a monosyllable vocabulary? A woman with limited education? A down-on-her-luck broad whose only witty repartee was most likely, 'Hey, buddy, need a tow?' Or maybe you thought I didn't probe you about your nickname because I couldn't possible understand the difference between catharsis and Katarthis. Between an emotional release and an avatar, no doubt created as part of an RPG."

Kat was stunned. He hadn't expected such a bitter diatribe, but more surprising, he hadn't expected her to be right.

For several moments the only sounds filling the truck were the slap of the wipers and the growl of the plow. He relented first.

"Gee," he murmured. "I sure messed that up. Should have gone with my other pickup line: 'What's a hot honey like you doin' drivin' a truck?'"

Apparently, Tam appreciated a good comeback. Her laughter was deep and unabashed. "Okay, you have a sense of humor. You're forgiven. I'm not usually so touchy about my profession," she added. "It's the long hours."

Again, Kat spoke without thinking. "The pay must be good to make you accept a job like this, eh?"

She shot him a warning glance; then shook her head. "Careful, Katman. That's a dangerous prejudice you're carting around." Gripping the wheel tightly, she threw a switch on the dashboard. Yellow lights began to rotate on the cab's roof, throwing caution beacons into the night. "What have we here?" she mumbled to herself.

Kat swung his head toward the road. Two sputtering emergency flares marked the spot where a man hunkered down next to his car, a tire iron in his hands.

"A flat?" he asked.

"Looks that way." Tamara bit her lip and tipped her head toward the motorist. "Can your lift to the hospital wait long enough for me to help?"

Kat thought about James pacing a hallway alone. But his friend was in a warm place, surrounded by professionals. The guy on the highway was in the cold surrounded by a blizzard of trouble. "If we both lend a hand, we'll get going again that much sooner."

Tam gave a quick nod, and swung open her door. Kat was right behind her.

Chapter *13*

If Kat had imagined himself the hero in this scenario, Tamara proved him wrong. She was far more efficient with a jack and tire iron than he. The damaged wheel was already lying on its side in the snow by the time he had removed the spare from the man's trunk.

"You far from home?" she shouted to the driver over the howling wind.

The man shook his head and shouted back. Kat couldn't hear him, but saw him point back toward High Street.

"The road is treacherous," she was shouting in return. "Maybe you should leave the car and come with us."

"He has chains in here," Kat yelled, gesturing at the open hatch.

Tam looked from Kat to the trunk and back. A raised eyebrow made her question clear.

"Yeah, I know how," he answered.

It took them about fifteen more minutes to spread the chains on the snow and coax the man's vehicle on top of them. Kat's fingers were tingling inside his gloves by the time they finished hooking them on, but the man's smile and wave as he drove off made it all worthwhile. With their hands buried deep in their coat pockets, the two Samaritans trotted back to the warmth of the truck.

Once inside, they yanked frozen fingers free of leather

coverings and held them up to the heat blasting from the vents. They laughed at their mutual desperation as they huffed off the cold.

"So," Tam said with a twinkle in her eye. "Where did a college-educated effete snob learn to attach snow chains so quickly—and so well, I might add?"

Kat had the good grace to blush. "Tractor, Farm and Fleet," he conceded. "I'm the manager. No college education," he confessed as well. "But guilty as charged on that effete snob thing. Is it too late for an apology?"

"None needed," she said, waving him off. "Attractive, funny, intelligent men are allowed one miscue with me—as long as they realize the error of their ways." With two jerks of the wrist, she lowered the plow to the road and shifted the truck into drive. "By the way, you can ask me now. You've earned an answer."

It took him a second to realize what she meant, but when he did, he was afraid to take her up on her offer.

"Really," she urged. "You're dying to know, so shoot."

Tam reached up, pulled a knit hat off her head and shook the snow off it onto the floor. Tossing it on the dash, she ran her fingers through her long auburn hair. Her resemblance to Ginie was stronger than ever. *To sleep, perchance to dream,* Kat thought. He had heard that somewhere before—and recently. As he gazed at Carole Tamara's striking face, the memory slipped away.

"How did you end up here?" he finally asked. "Tonight? When I needed you most?"

The expression the young woman turned on him was a mixture of pleasure and surprise. "That's better, Kat Petty. *Much* better." Her eyes slid off his face and back to the road. He missed her gaze the moment it left. "Well," she began. "Life put me here, I guess. Short version: I was only a so-so student in high school. Exceptional at some subjects. Hopeless at others." She paused to consider how much more to tell him, then with a decisive nod, she forged ahead. "The thing I failed at most miserably was saying no to a certain beautiful high school quarterback. When I told him of his impending fatherhood, we had a disagreement about the best way to rectify the situation. He took off for college to learn how to become a beautiful high school football coach. I dropped out of school to learn how to be a single mom."

Kat tried not to recoil but she picked up on his tension. "Don't worry," she said a bit sadly. "Parenthood is not catching."

"And the French?" he asked quickly, hoping to divert her disappointment in him.

She grinned. "What a straight line, Mr. Petty! I *could* say I learned it from the same beautiful quarterback. But the truth is my mother wanted her children to be bilingual. She spoke French and English to my sister and me from the moment we were born. Esther is older and speaks the language like a native. I think Mom got tired by the time I came along. I only know enough to show off."

Esther? he wondered.

"Esther?" he asked.

"Biblical-sounding, isn't it? And interesting. Not as interesting as Katarthis though. Actually, sis's name is a family heirloom. My grandmother was an Esther too."

Kat couldn't hold back his gasp. Tam didn't seem to hear it.

"Your parents must have been upset when you dropped out," he said to cover his reaction. "They must have hoped for so much more."

Tam rolled her head on stiffened shoulders. "'So much more'? More than a daughter who chose the right way instead of the easy way? More than a wonderful twelve-year-old granddaughter who they adore? Yeah, I'm sure you're right."

"You know that's not what I meant. More for *you*. More opportunities. More experiences. More diversity and culture in your life."

Tam slammed on the brake and the flying rooster tail of snow plummeted to the ground. She shifted the truck into park and turned sideways in her seat, pulling one knee up onto the torn upholstery. "Actually, I *don't* know what you meant because I don't know *you*. I thought at first I would like to, but almost every word that leaves your mouth convinces me I should dump you and run for the hills." She leaned in close, her eyes a crackling fire. "More opportunities? I own my own business and it turns a profit. I know more about the inside of an engine then any three mechanics at the local dealership—and they come to me for advice. Not to mention, they ask for a date now and then. More experiences? I work with my Grandpa Jack who is funny, loving, and brilliant with a socket wrench. No college degree there either but who cares? He's the smartest, bravest man I know. When Grandma Esther died, he upped and moved twenty hours northwest into a frozen land he knew nothing about and started over from scratch. More diversity? More culture? I create hammered-silver jewelry—original designs that I sell online. I write poetry. My house is filled with books from my late Grandma Esther, watercolors from my late Nana Azrael, and old albums by French folksingers from her husband, my not-so-late Grandpapa Rafe. My father is a banker who taught me the value of a dollar—and how little it is worth when compared to the value of family. My mother is a stay-at-home parent who can spout Beowulf better than a Cambridge scholar. I have a lively daughter who loves me. And more importantly, I love myself. But you're right," she concluded with a sharp finger to his chest. "I probably could use a little more of *something* in my life. But when I figure out what it is, I'll get it for myself, thank you very much."

Carole Tamara leaned across Kat's lap and hit the handle of his door with the heel of her hand. "What I don't need," she said in a now calmer voice, "is a self-righteous prig who I've known less than forty minutes telling me what he thinks I am missing."

Kat inhaled deeply as the young woman straightened and turned forward to face the road. Her hair smelled of grapefruits and honey—a scent he would most likely never enjoy again. Or ever forget. The wind outside his open door sucked it away, leaving him desolate.

Had he learned nothing tonight?

"I'm so sorry, Tam," he began softly. "I am a prig. And a dolt. And a bitter thirty-four-year-old wish-I'd-been. I should know better. There are things I wanted to do with my life too, but didn't. We don't always have a choice, do we? Survival dictates what paths we take. Who am I to judge?"

The woman wouldn't look his way. She stared out at the swirling snow and shook her head. "Hmmph," she exhaled through her nose. "Define the requirements for survival, Kat. Perhaps I did give up one path—or many possible paths—in order to accept my responsibilities. Perhaps you did too. But what we did, we did knowingly. There is always a choice. I'm sorry you're not happy with yours."

She leaned forward and peered up at something in the sky above the truck. "Right this moment," she said thoughtfully, "I choose not to feel bad about myself. Despite the fact that we might have had a lot in common and could have enjoyed some interesting times together, I choose to let you out and never look back."

Kat dragged his eyes away from her profile and toward the point in the sky that held her attention. **ST. STEPHEN'S**

HOSPITAL glowed red on a white sign above their heads.

"Good-bye, Jasper Petty," Carole Tamara McShirin said. "Have a good life."

Chapter *14*

Kat stood in the cold watching the truck's taillights disappear into the storm. When his Da died sixteen years before, had Kat really made a choice? He had always felt otherwise—that changes in his life had not been chosen, but had been thrust upon him. Hadn't his mother needed him? Hadn't his college money been better spent keeping her in the home she had shared with the man she loved?

An image of his mother's carefully decorated parlor materialized in his mind, more a mausoleum than a celebration of life. Had she done it for the man she'd loved and lost—or for the son who'd helped trap her in the past? "If I had gone to college, would she have sold the house and moved on with her life?" *Would she have met a new love sooner rather than later?*

A strong gust of wind whined around his ears and Kat shivered. Had she made the choice to stay a widow in that old home because Kat Petty had made the choice to sacrifice his dreams to keep her there?

Jack McShirin's spouse had died too. But his son Noel had not given up everything to take care of the parent who'd been left behind.

"You don't know for sure that Noel is Tam's father," he muttered to himself.

The wind chided him again. Of course he did. Just as he knew Noel had married Ginie. That he had found his dream career in the country's heartland. Had convinced Ginie to leave college and join him there.

"No. Ginie wouldn't have needed persuading," he corrected himself. She would have known what Jack knew, and Esther knew, and Noel knew, and Tam knew. You have to grab at life's chances for happiness when they come your way. The choice is always yours.

The truck had been gone for quite awhile now but Kat continued to stare after it. Had he just made another disastrous decision?

There was no time to consider the answer. James was inside waiting for him. Needing him. Right now, Kat would do what he could for his friend. Later, he would do what he could for Kat Petty

D.L. Meyer & Valia Kapadai

Chapter 15

Kat entered the glass doors and stomped the snow from his boots. A tiny nun with a halo of curls looked up from the information desk.

"Lolita Pelmutter?" he asked.

The woman gave him a piercing stare from under her short white veil. "Friend or family?"

"Family," he lied.

The maternity ward was on the third floor. She made no mention of Lolly's condition. Did he imagine the pained expression on her face?

Kat road the elevator to level three and stepped out uncertainly. There was something unsettling about being in a ward filled with women celebrating life's greatest miracle. Especially if you were a single male who had not yet been invited to the party.

A second nun pointed him down the hall to a dark lounge. James Pelmutter, she said, was in there, waiting for further news. Again, Kat thought he saw pain in the woman's quickly downcast eyes.

As Kat approached, a doctor in green surgical scrubs stepped out of an intersecting hall and turned in front of him. The man moved slowly, a half-dozen steps ahead, his shoulders slumped, his head bowed.

Lolly's doctor.

Kat knew it without question and his heart sank.

In the darkness of the lounge at the end of the hall, he could just make out the shadows of two people. One, a large man, was slumped forward in a chair, his face in his hands: James. The other, Kat thought at first, was a slim woman with long blonde hair. She was leaning over Jim from behind, her arms wrapped around his chest.

It was only when the doctor entered and James leaped to his feet that Kat saw the woman was Chi.

"Doctor?" he heard Jim whisper.

Whatever was about to be said was between a husband and the man caring for his wife. Kat tarried in the hall to give them privacy. Chi looked his way, then stepped out from behind the chair and engulfed James once more in his arms.

There was a long whispered exchange. James staggered. Chi kept him on his feet. The doctor placed a hand on Jim's shoulder and patted it twice. Kat fought down an urge to scream. The man in the surgical scrubs faltered, and then turned away. He passed Kat without notice, his eyes weary and sad.

James stood in the middle of the lounge staring at the floor. As Kat stepped into the doorway, he spoke his friend's name. Jim's head snapped up and Chi released him from his embrace. With a gentle push, the man in black passed James from one pair of arms to another.

"Kat! Oh God, Kat. You made it. You came." Big strong James Pelmutter shuddered against Kat's chest like a lost child. His tears dampened Kat's cheek. His sobs rocked them back and forth. "I knew I could count on you."

"Hush, hush," Kat crooned. It didn't sound one bit foolish. "I'm here. Tell me what you need. Tell me what I can do."

James sucked in a deep swallow of air and finally pushed away. "You already did it," he moaned. "You got here."

Kat led him back to the chair; then pulled another seat away from the wall so he could sit down facing his friend. Whatever he was going to hear, whatever would have to be said or done, he would do it. He was an old hand at sacrifices. What was one or two more? If he had looked up he would have seen Chi hovering nearby, a frown creasing his forehead.

"What did the doctor say?" Kat asked, expecting the worse.

"It was an abruptio placenta," James said slowly, being careful to pronounce the words as he had heard them. "Part of the placenta tore away from the uterus. Lolly was bleeding. Bleeding everywhere. It wouldn't stop. I got her a towel, and we got in the car to come right here. But the weather..." James halted to gulp more air. "She kept getting weaker. And the blood soaked through her clothes. Through the towel. Onto the car seat." He shuddered again and Kat took hold of his friend's large hands. "It took so long to get here, she went into shock. Started shivering and wouldn't talk to me. They just lifted her onto a gurney and rushed her to surgery."

James stopped speaking and Kat squeezed his fingers.

"What did the doctor say, Jim? Tell me. Let me help."

James Pelmutter looked up from their clasped hands and sighed. "An emergency C section. The baby was in distress. His heartbeat was fading. They did what they could. Took him uterus and all. Started transfusions for Lolly. Called for a pediatric specialist. The baby wasn't breathing. Lolly was unconscious." His voice stuttered to a stop again.

Kat reminded himself to stay calm. To not cry.

"The baby is going to make it, Kat. Reggie is okay. A big boy: nine pounds, twenty-one inches. Strong. I can see him in a little while."

Kat had forgotten to inhale, and couldn't make himself do so now.

"Lolly is weak, but getting better. I can see her too."

James shook his big head. "We won't be able to have any more children, Kat. I have to tell her that. In a few minutes. They are moving her into recovery."

Kat's heart kicked into gear and the oxygen he'd been denying himself filled his lungs. "Aw, Jim, I am so sorry."

"What do I say? How do I tell her? She wanted a big family. It's all she's ever talked about."

A shadow fell across James's shoulder. The man in the black wrinkled suit looked down at Kat, waiting patiently. And in that moment, the lessons finally fell into place.

Kat stood up and pulled his gentle giant of a friend to his feet. "It's easy, Jim." He let go of his hands and stepped to his side, slipping an arm around his shoulder and leading him toward the door. "You hug her. You hug her as tight as the doctor will allow. You kiss her," he added as he steered him into the hall. "And you hover over her the way you always do."

James slowed and pursed his lips. "I do not hover."

"You do," Kat said with a grin. "You hover and you should never stop."

A woman with long shiny auburn hair and sable eyes was standing near the nurses' station. Kat saw her, but couldn't stop speaking now if his life depended on it—which he feared it did.

"You tell her that you love her, and that no matter what else has happened tonight, you feel like the luckiest man alive."

James looked startled but he grabbed hold of Kat's wrist, trusting his friend to give him the help he had been seeking when he called him out into the storm.

"Because it's true, James Pelmutter," Kat told him. "You have the woman you love and the family you both wanted. There is nothing luckier than that."

Jim nodded, and began to turn away. He stopped one last

time, looked back and scratched his head. "Won't she cry?"

Kat nodded and grinned. "Yep. She sure will. I can't help you there, buddy. That's your department."

James grinned too, and stepped away with more confidence than Kat had seen since arriving on the scene. Chi slipped past to follow him.

"Nice job," the man in black said, applauding loudly as he left. "Now, are you ready to take your own advice?"

Carole Tamara McShirin approached slowly. Was she really there? Or just Kat's own wishful thinking?

"You came back," he said to her.

"Me? Nah, I just happened to be passing through."

"Through the maternity ward?"

She grinned, and propped a fist on a jaunty oh-so-desirable hip. "Uh-huh. Through the first floor. Then through the second floor. And then the third floor."

When he wrinkled his forehead, she bit her lip. "Well, come on. What was a girl supposed to do? You didn't say why you were coming here or who you were going to see."

His face cleared. "If there had been a fourth and a fifth floor—or twenty floors, would you have kept looking?"

"Probably. I'm pretty sure. Yes." Now she looked embarrassed and Kat wanted to crush her in his arms.

"You were going to dump me and run for the hills," he insisted. "Maybe you still should."

Carole Tamara McShirin looked him up and down boldly. "I got to thinking. You apologized so nicely. And maybe you were attractive enough and intelligent enough to deserve one of my very rare third chances."

Kat stepped to her side, cradled her elbow in his palm and turned her toward the elevator. "I won't need a fourth," he promised.

As they waited for the doors to open, Chi stuck his head out of the recovery room in time to hear their next exchange.

"Why 'Kat'?" she asked.

"It was my fantasy super-hero name when I was a kid. Half dragon, half man. I wrote a short story about it once and won ten-thousand dollars."

"You're a writer?" she asked, excitement building in her voice.

"Yep. When I'm not marking down snow shovels."

The elevator arrived and they stepped inside.

"Why 'Tam'?" he asked.

The doors closed.

The man in the black suit smiled. He didn't have to hear the rest. After all, he'd written the script. He shook his head and turned back toward the recovery room.

"She just never saw herself as a Carole."

About the Author

Denise Meyer has been writing professionally for over 27 years, initially as a magazine editor, then as an ad agency creative director, and currently as a marketing copywriter for *The Blade* newspaper in Toledo, Ohio. She admits to finding inspiration for her stories in the wisecracks of her effusive daughter, sardonic son, droll son-in-law, comical grandchildren, and a host of fictional "houseguests" who don't know they are fictional, and thus are equally hilarious. For more about the recent Meyer novel *Fellowship of Psys,* visit www.fellowshipofpsys.com.

About the Illustrator

Valia Kapadai [aka Valium] is a full-time dreamer and a comic junkie. She's currently working as a graphic designer and illustrator at the University of Athens in the morning, while she turns into a watercolour-thirsty creature by night, mostly drawing comic pages. She loves spending her little free time with her love and inspiration, Kostas, their cat Yuki, beloved family and friends, comics and music. Usually lost inside her own messy world, she can also be found all over the place and in a webpage near you: http://neurotic-elf.deviantart.com

About the Story

Not Another Christmas Carole is the first Meyer-Kapadai collaboration. With a respectful nod to Charles Dickens, it is based on the true-life traumas of a Meyer friend who lost hope one Christmas when yet another of his girlfriends left him on yet another rainy day. The author and illustrator are happy to say, this "Kat" and his "Carole" now live happily ever after. It's all about the chi.

www.ingramcontent.com/pod-product-compliance
Lightning Source LLC
Chambersburg PA
CBHW050831180626
46814CB00004B/1573